Dusty and the Cowboy

Rendezvous

Dusty and the Cowboy

Rendezvous

T. W. Lawrence

Study Guide by
Jonathan Cooper

Published by Luckenbach Press

First Printing
Study Guide Edition

ISBN: 978-0-9889605-6-5

Dedication

This anthology is dedicated to all those who trudge on their personal journey; some days battered, some days praised, but never quitting the trail.

Acknowledgments

If I've learned nothing else in these last few months, it's that writing a book is not something done alone.

I would like to express my heartfelt appreciation for those who helped make me look so good on paper:

My editor: Fran Lawrence
My cover artist: Vanessa Lowry
My production coordinator: Jessica Parker
My publisher: Luckenbach Press

Special thanks to Michael Belk for his great photo used on the front cover. To see more of his work and the path he is now taking, please visit:

www.journeyswiththemessiah.com.

Thank you all,
T.W. Lawrence

Table of Contents

Introduction

I never expected *Dusty and the Cowboy* to get this far. But, at the same time I've come to understand that I'm not the One in charge.

From its unheralded inclusion as a filler piece to round out an anthology of Texas tales, the original story of "Dusty" took on a life of its own. Feedback determined that this story was the beginning of something.

That something turned out to be *The Cowboy Trilogy*. In the beginning there was only the intention to complete a single book. *Dusty and the Cowboy: Lord Show Me The Way* did that.

Stopping there would have been a worthy accomplishment, but then I heard my pastor give a sermon that I just knew was directed solely at me. It was about how each Christian actually has three stories: 1) before knowing the Savior, 2) committing to Christ. and 3) life after knowing the Lord.

Sitting in the pew that Sunday, I knew that Cowboy's story had to follow along the lines of that lesson. In this current volume, *Dusty and the Cowboy: Rendezvous*, the main character continues along his journey. He comes to discover that the purpose of his travels is not the one he started out with. He learns that it goes much deeper. By the book's end Cowboy knows what he must do and what part his faith must play in it.

More exciting to me, personally, is how the books in the series are being increasingly used by both Cowboy Churches and mainstream denominations as resources for Men's Bible Study.

Cowboy's journey will continue in the third and final volume. In the tradition of great classical journeys, the story ends with the prodigal coming home. There are yet more lessons for Cowboy to learn along the way. I hope the journey takes you there, too.

From the outset, I believed that the trilogy must be recorded as an audiobook. Some of the intended audience likes to listen rather than read, and I wanted this work to reach them as well.

I was fortunate to be introduced to Country Hall of Fame DJ, Moby, star of the Moby in the Morning Show. He took an immediate liking to the stories. We have become friends as well as collaborators on this project. He recently shared with me how he viewed the series. "It really feels like I'm looking over Cowboy's shoulder, narrating his life. Seeing what he sees. Feeling what he feels. I love doing this...There's a spiritual message from beginning to the end of this. I think these stories are good."

My hope is that you think so, too.

T.W. Lawrence

Cattle Trails

A Word Given

"Ray's dead."

Those few words, and the long silence that followed, were all the warning Cowboy got that his old friend had unexpectedly passed over. That jolt of ill tidings staggered the wrangler. Like being sucker-punched hard in the ribs, Cowboy found it tough to draw next breath. He felt his insides clench up, gripped by some unseen hand. For many years Ray Patterson, in close partnership with his pretty wife Esmeralda, had owned the tidy boarding house next door and that white-washed horse barn, in which Cowboy was now standing holding Dusty by the reins. The buildings sat squat on the rise just before the trail went down into Cowtown.

Cowboy guessed the man staring back at him stone-faced and still as a monument was the current, albeit much less affable, proprietor. "His woman sold me this place four days after they put him in the ground," the man said. "Then I heard she went back to her people in New Mexico, somewhere near that big pueblo east of Santa Fe."

The old man resembled an aging Percheron stallion: barrel of a chest, thick through the belly, and stout across the haunches. Thin white hairs of uneven length poked out from the brim of his snap-brim hat. "Folks 'round here complain I speak too plain," he said. But Cowboy heard no apology in his voice. "Don't mince," the man continued. "Just say what I say straight-forward. On occasion," he begrudged, "wife calls it hurtsome and rude. Took you for just another drifter about to tell me some hard luck yarn about life in the saddle and trying to natter a free meal out of me. And some feed for his horse, too." The man's protruding lip indicated how unlikely that would be. "Name's John Dowling." The man did not extend his hand to the tall stranger. Instead, he stood flatfooted, struggling to match Cowboy's unflinching gaze. "That look on your face just now," the man said at last. "Patterson must have meant something to you. He kith or kin?"

Words did not come to Cowboy the first time he tried. He had to swallow hard, twice, just to wet his mouth enough to speak. "Ray and me was pards from way back" Cowboy answered in a tone too weak to be characteristic of him. "First time I ever pushed cattle north from Texas, he was the only drover in the outfit to take me under his wing. I was still just a boy compared to them other punchers, but Ray kept me from hurting myself when I'd do something stupid with the beeves or the horses." Cowboy felt a rush of warmth roll down his neck and back recalling those many foibles. "Truth be told, I owe that man my life, on more than one occasion."

"When you last seen him?" Dowling asked, ignoring the Texan's brief struggle with reminiscence and grief.

"Three years come August," Cowboy said, composed once more. "Last time I brought a herd across the Pedernales. Stayed here two days. He seemed fit as a yearling then."

"Boarding house not the place I'd expect a passel of trail hands to bed down, when the lures of Cowtown are so close."

"Oh, I'd visit Ray and Essie, as he called her, while the boys whooped it up in town after the cattle sold and we got our money."

"Put you up with the paying boarders did he?"

Cowboy imagined that if Dowling had been wearing a money belt around his ample bib-and-brace dungarees at that moment, he'd be clutching it close. Using both hands. "Not like that at all," he said. "The lone place I ever slept on this whole property is in that hayloft behind you." Cowboy pointed over Dowling's head. "And that was only after Ray'd worked me hard enough to earn leftover vittles from that day's table fare. Once't, I pitched a wagon's worth of silage into that loft in the span of an afternoon. Another, I cut a whole load of saw-milled lumber to length so we could put up that shed out back. Last time, I shimmied up the windmill tower to replace two broken blades and unbend that crooked throw rod. Made Essie's cooking taste that much better." Cowboy slid into another fond reverie at the thought of her. "Ham and biscuits were my favorite. That lady could cook anything from scratch."

Cowboy turned away from Dowling now. He took the time to sweep his look across the barn in all directions. Stalls had been recently cleaned, but not today. Tack and equipment hung in place by rows. And the only two bags of feed stood stacked squarely in a corner. This, Cowboy judged, was work done by other hands. Dowling's clean finger nails and unsoiled clothing suggested that, but his hat's absence of sweat stains confirmed it. Without question, the man seemed to wheeze with every word spoken, more deeply even with the mildest exertion. And though Dowling disguised it with a fresh juniper sliver clenched between his teeth, the sourness of some fermented brew wafted over Cowboy every time the man spoke.

"Ain't seen your hired man since I rode up today," Cowboy said. "What manner of chore you got him on?"

"Not a thing." Dowling replied. His lower lip thrust out once more, this time joined by the thick upper one as well. He held his face as though sucking a lump of lemon sour candy. "He's gone. Lit out this morning, right after I paid his wage. Wasn't long after he read that letter I handed him, along with the money, that he yelled out, 'Oh Caroline' and threw his few belongings in an old war bag. Minutes later, he'd saddled that skinny pony of his and galloped out of town, headed north." Dowling stared at the toes of his work boots. "Like as not, I've seen the last of Billy Mitchell."

At this unexpected turn of events, Cowboy nodded — more to himself than to Dowling. "See-ins you're a man short and still got chores aplenty, I say we parlay. There's a wagon's load of uncut timbers outside needs chopped to firewood. I don't for the life of me see you doing that yourself."

"Give you same arrangement as Ray did, I guess: loft for a bed and meal fixin's every day," the old man said with a straight face.

"Naw," Cowboy replied. "I don't owe you same as I done him." His eyes began to twinkle. "Looks like Billy Mitchell give you good effort in all he done. What deal was it you strike with him?"

"Same as I just said," Dowling replied. "Except five U.S. dollars paid in coin at each month's end." He bit his jaws hard together after he spoke, almost but not quite managing to make his eyes go neutral.

"Looks like that deal couldn't keep him here," Cowboy said. "You'd sooner catch rattlesnakes eating from berry bushes than see me work for such little as that." He smiled, and took his time folding the leather gloves in his hand before shoving them into a coat pocket. "No matter. I'll stay to Sunday next, do what needs doing in the barn. I'll split your wood and stack it too. Cost you three dollars plus that other." He shifted his weight toward Dowling. "Fair enough?"

Dowling nodded one time without hesitation, punctuating the agreement with a loud harrumph. He took two steps to go around Cowboy on the way to the boarding house, when Cowboy stopped him. "I was brought up to handshake a deal when it's struck. Let the other fella know, when you look him in the eye, that you'd keep your word." He held his big hand out to Dowling.

The old man, for his part, moved in closer and raised a thick palm to his face. With a pop of dry air from his puckered mouth, Dowling pretended to spit in his hand and shook Cowboy's. As Dowling stepped back, tall puncher asked him, "You must be Amish?"

"Was," Dowling said and walked out of the barn.

The balance of the afternoon allowed the time for Cowboy to ease himself from trail rider back to a working hand once more. He unsaddled Dusty, throwing the blanket, rig, and bridle over the wood of the closest stall. Cowboy took his time with the groom's brush he'd found, giving the horse's neck, back, and legs a thorough going-over. He spent extra time brushing any spot matted down by sweat and rubbing leather. Then Cowboy settled into to doing Dowling's work, starting with the stalls.

Not that the choice mattered much, Cowboy found himself once again humming a long forgotten ditty from his childhood. "Green Grow the Lilacs" now was mostly sung by the old-timers, particularly those who believed that song begat the term "gringo". The Professor had once assured Cowboy the name actually started in Spain, and besides Cowboy was rarely called that name to his face any more. His most immediate concern was where to put the horse droppings he'd finished raking into a small heap. The compost pile Ray carefully maintained out back had disappeared. Essie had used it with such success in her tidy cottage garden. Weeds and rabbit grass now stood in place of her herbs and tomatoes.

In one breath, then two, and finally a third, Cowboy recognized that some new scent had swirled around him on the breeze. The wind blew through the double doors facing to the east, made its way across the barn's length, before funneling out through a set of Dutch windows high on the back wall. Now, mixed with the smell of hay and horse manure, he could detect a distinct whiff of roses. Cowboy could remember that bouquet in particular from the big clump of yellow ones in front of his home place in Atacosa County. His mother pampered them there every spring.

Turning where he stood with pitchfork in hand, Cowboy stopped when he saw the girl. Eighteen years he guessed, and recognized that she would be quite the beauty in her majority. She stood tallish. Long braids hung bound together by a thin slip of lace. They swept around the neck and down one shoulder, dangling past her apron's top. The dress of threadbare calico matched her well-worn leather footwear. But the apron appeared, to Cowboy, to center her utmost attention and pride. A homespun cloth extending past the knees, it easily stretched across the narrow hips. Along its edges, hand-sewn threads were needled into floral decoration, with the most elaborate embellishments looping across the apron's bib. Such stitching evidenced a talented skillful woman. One with much time on her hands.

Cowboy did not see the resemblance in her face, but asked just the same, "You old man Dowling's daughter?"

"For a fact, I am not," she said. Her eyes, a watchful pecan-brown, held Cowboys own in a stare that seemed to bore right through him. It held an equal mix of caution and curiosity. "Lydia Dowling, currently his wife, is my mother's oldest sister. I'm Emma Sanford." She closed the gap between them by taking three small strides. "And who, sir, might you be?"

Her direct dealing and steadfast manner made Cowboy like this Emma instantly. In one hand she held a tin plate full of dumplings and some side meat and in the other a folded cloth containing small chunks of day-old bread. He could smell those too, now that she was close.

"Guess best way's said, I'm the new man been given charge of barn, stock, and feed. Stalls got my attention to begin with, as you can see from this pile."

"New?" she burst the question at him. "What have you done with Billy Mitchell?"

"Can't say, miss. Never laid eyes on him myself. Only heard tell." Cowboy set the pitchfork aside and squared himself to watch the girl more fully. Her face had begun to flush in some agitation. "From what old Dowling spoke of this morning," Cowboy continued, "it seems the fella throws kit and kaboodle across a horse and hightails it outta here in one big sweat."

With a calmness that masked her growing unease, Emma placed the tin and cloth atop a stout wooden bin at her Feet. She all but brushed Cowboy out of her way as she hurried to the tack room door at the barn's rear corner. It opened on noisy dead-nail hinges.

Sixty long seconds of fretful silence, Emma stood in the shadowed doorway, one hand on the jamb, the other clinging the latch. In the afternoon's failing light, she could feel more than see the room's emptiness of everything Billy Mitchell. Gone was the bedroll from the narrow cot. Gone too were jacket and denims once hung on a cedar peg. No folded razor, no pocket watch on the shelf; just gathered ranch implements and leathers left behind when Ray's wife sold out to Emma's uncle.

Cowboy stood without a word, watching the girl's head shake slowly side to side, chin to her chest. He had no sister, and at this age no daughter, to judge the pain and disappointment he now was a witness to. Like watching a crippled calf being swarmed by coyotes, his heart began to pain.

She re-closed the flimsy door. To its rough uneven surface she spoke out low, "Billy Mitchell, you are a weakling and a liar." No tears fell; only the muffled choke of her hard swallow could be heard before she went on. "You broke the one promise you swore you'd always keep."

In such a disposition, Emma turned to see Cowboy as if for the first time. She quickly recovered, but defeat still clung to her pretty features. To him she said, "You're doing the work now, so I suppose that supper's yours. Leave the plate on the stoop and I'll see you get fed breakfast too." In a moment she was through the barn's huge open doors.

"Evening, Miss Sanford," Cowboy told the retreating figure, touching his hat's brim. Bringing his full attention then to the still empty tack room compartment he said, "Billy Mitchell, I pray our paths shall cross one day soon." Fingers of one big hand tightened to a ball. "I have a fist full of uncried tears to bring you, *su cobarde*. You coward. Then maybe your tally page in Emma's ledger won't be so deep in the hole."

He flipped the cloth back on the bundle sitting next to the plate. Taking the largest chunk of darkened bread, Cowboy walked to Dusty's stall. The horse had watched the goings-on as well, his head and neck extended over the stall's short gate. Cowboy fed the piece to Dusty and stroked the ears while thinking still of Billy. "The boy was reared all wrong, *compadre*," he said. "Living out here a man should know, for any pard you'd trust to ride the river with, keep your word above all else. That's even in the Bible."

* * *

The air stayed cool that morning even under a cloudless sky. Sun had just begun to filter over the tops of Dowling's house and barn. But, Cowboy could begin to feel a warmer trace that would only increase along these rolling plains in coming days.

He sat leaned back against the buckboard's box seat. One boot rested propped against the brake handle. Cowboy seldom wasted time. Even as he sat waiting for the ladies of the house, he pulled the hardback from his coat and began to read.

Both horses of his team stood silent, with little movement, in their leather collar and tugs. Occasionally, one or the other would give its hide a shake, bob and snort, or paw at some rock in the dirt with a hoof.

Through the curtained window nearest him, the one facing out across the covered porch, Cowboy heard the mantle clock begin to chime the coming hour. Before the count came halfway done, Emma Sanford stepped through the door. Cowboy grinned on the inside. He'd already judged her to value timeliness as much as she did the detail of her sewing.

The book he jammed back in his coat pocket, finding that it almost didn't fit on the first try. "Morning, miss," Cowboy said with a touch of the hat, as he slid from seat to ground. He extended his palm up, for her to use or not, as she reached for the mounting step. Emma took his hand. "And to you, sir," she said, flashing a smile that verged on true merriment. She caught him glancing at the door with puzzled anticipation as he untied the team from their weighted horse tether.

When Cowboy did not immediately return to his post on the wagon seat, Emma said, "My aunt's not coming, if that's what you're waiting for. She doesn't feel well. It will be just you and me this morning." So, Cowboy clambered into the wagon beside her and unwound the reins from the brake handle.

He saw the smile again and thought how different that looked from her expression just two nights ago, the last time he'd actually seen her. Her dress was different, too. Just as old as the other; grey not calico. No apron, but a small bonnet sat atop her upswept hair, held there by a substantial hat pin of some antiquity. Cowboy judged it to be a valued heirloom. Its length was that or longer than the knife he wore sheathed at his hip.

"Are you always so formal?" She asked.

"Tradition, miss." Cowboy agreed. "Leastwise, the way Mama raised us boys. Proper conduct when ladies was present." He let that hang.

"She did a fine job," Emma said. "Which is more than I can say for my own kin. Today, you carry an unchaperoned young woman of a certain age to the heart of the ill-reputed Cowtown and return her home." She stopped only to catch her breath. "By yourself mind you. So either they trust you without question, having known you less than three days – or perhaps they think I'm not worth the worry."

Cowboy studied Emma's features before reply. He began to smile. "I 'spect with your frank speaking and direct manner, you're more likely to air out a man's liver two or three times with that stout silver pin of yours than put up with anything untoward." His smile broadened. "Comes down to it, miss, I'm the one needs protecting here."

That drew her laughter. "I swear I won't stick you if you'll just call me Emma.

Cowboy let the horses bump the wagon along at an easy gait. "Sorry to hear your aunt's feeling so poorly. It's a fine day for a ride in the fresh air."

"W-e-l-l," Emma exaggerated that one syllable. "Today, she has the vapors, or is it her lumbago? I can't remember." She shrugged with the slightest movement of her shoulders. "It might be that dyspepsia again or maybe the gout. No, wait, that was last week. Doesn't matter. Whatever the infirmity, it seems to keep her chair-bound most of the day, leaving all the cleanup and cooking to me." She looked at Cowboy with widened eyes filled with false earnestness. "She does, however, manage to recover in time to sit at the table for mealtime."

An unseen rut caught a lead wheel hard enough to jerk the wagon sideways. The two passengers pitched in their seats, bouncing them together. Cowboy slapped the reins hard to keep the rig from bogging down in the rough patch.

"If you don't mind my asking, Emma," Cowboy ventured. "They're not your maw and pa, so why are you living here? Have your folks passed on?"

"No," Emma answered. "That was just the first betrayal. More and more I find that people don't keep their word." She dared him with her look. "Do you?"

Without taking his eyes off the road or the team, Cowboy simply said, "A word given is a promise kept." He turned to find Emma watching him intently. He said, "What double-dealing have you endured?"

"After they bought the place, my aunt and uncle found that it was more than they could handle. My parents sent me here to lend a hand until they could settle in and find good help. 'A year at most they said.' That was almost three years ago." Her jaw set more in determination than resignation. "My entreaties to my folks have been answered only with equivocation. So, I'm left to cook and clean and sew. I'd call that a broken promise."

"You said 'first'. Were there others?" Cowboy asked.

"Uncle John and Aunt Lydia told me that I would be just like the daughter they never had. We'd be as close as my real family." That thought produced a half-smile. "Indentured servitude should have ended when General Washington defeated the Redcoats, but I'm living proof that it's still alive and well. A second promise shattered."

"How's Billy Mitchell figure into all this?" Cowboy asked.

"He's just the latest." Her tone turned flat. "Knew when he said it, he didn't mean it. Billy swore that when he finally left this place, he'd take me with him." She gave a weak laugh. "It still hurt when he left alone. A promise is a promise."

And still no tears came. Emma looked out at the uneven wave of open prairie, absent of any trees too tall. But her eyes focused on nothing. She said, "Folks breaking a promise are lying to you, but not to your face. Like being cut with a knife, except you don't feel the pain 'till the betrayal comes to light. Hard to trust anyone after enough of them do it, especially family." She looked at her hands for a moment. "I don't know which is worse, the fact that the promise was a lie or that I believed them."

After a pause Cowboy asked, "You figure to marry Billy, or just take up with him?"

"Not like that at all." Emma said a bit more lively. "He wanted to go back to Littlefield, where he came from, once he'd gotten over this girl who broke his heart. Said he could work in the feed store there. Since I'm good with figures, I could get on with the bank or I could cook at the railroad café." She looked at Cowboy with impish eyes. "You didn't tell me about the letter Billy got or mention this Caroline. No wonder he left in such haste. I was just dirt on his boots."

For long moment the only the rhythmic grating of the kingbolt holding the harness fast to the wagon and the accompanying creak of seat springs broke the silence.

"When I peeked out the curtains, just before the clock rang, I saw you reading something. What was it, a dime novel or some penny western?" She asked.

"No, miss, it was my Bible."

"You're a Christian then?" Emma asked as though she'd never seen one this close up before.

"Mostly," Cowboy responded.

"I thought you either were or you weren't. What makes you say it that way?"

"I got a younger brother, Marcus," Cowboy said. "Who's a preacher back home. Has the faith like no man I ever seen. Couldn't bend it with railroad steel." His eyes filled with wonder at the thought of it. "I'm not there yet. Truth is, I don't give it my full attention. And there are things I got to work out in my mind first." He looked relieved to tell her. "Sorta why me and Dusty are headed up the trail. Something I got to do first."

Emma saw the brown leather corner jutting out from the coat pocket. "Where would I read in there about promises being kept?" She pointed to the book.

"You tell me," Cowboy said. He wrestled out the hardback and handed it to her as he spoke. "I'll be sure to get it back when I take my leave, end of the week. Till then, it's yours to read over. Start wherever you will and give it a go."

Emma looked at the book now in her lap like it was some flat-tailed horny toad, but she made no protest. Neither did she give it back.

Before more could be said, Cowboy reined in the horses at the town limit sign. Cowtown had changed some since his last visit, more mercantile stores than he remembered. "Where should I let you off?" He asked. "Won't take that long for me to load up your uncle's freight delivery at the depot. Be back before you know it."

Emma directed him to the large store standing in the midst of a long block of wooden buildings. She took a paper from her dress pocket and patted the coins in there. It was part of her ritual that began the coming haggle with shopkeepers over the list of goods she needed. This was the sheer pleasure in her otherwise monotonous living.

* * *

The bustle of the big city did not sit well with Cowboy's contemplative nature. Throngs of townspeople, numbering as many as three abreast, crossed the rutted street in front of the buckboard carefully stepping around manure mounds. They all seemed to be talking at once, each voice raised to be heard over the others. The number of mounted riders making their way to and fro, bound for places Cowboy could not fathom, greatly exceeded that needed to push any large herd from here to Montana. Their shouts to one another only added to the general din. The quantity of buggies, surreys, shays, and carts was more than Cowboy cared to count. Cowtown was anything but quiet.

The clamor only increased as Cowboy and his team neared the train station with the freight depot nearby. Metal striking metal around the locomotive, wood on wood as freight boxes were shoved along the loading dock. Cowboy longed for the stillness of the trail, where the only sound was the blowing wind and Dusty's footfalls on the ground. He waited with reins in hand for a somewhat large freight wagon, stacked high with oak barrels lashed together, to leave the loading dock. Four pair of stout horses strained and puffed to pull that load.

Cowboy saw that his mild annoyance with the city sounds was more that matched by the wiry grey pony a young man was struggling to tie to a hitching post in front of the depot office. Ears back flat, eyes darting wildly, the horse jerked hard at the reins in an effort to get himself away from there - to no avail. Cowboy judged the young rider to be quite the horseman, if he had the boldness to bring such an excitable animal into all this commotion. The man carried himself well, had handsome strong features, and seemed dressed neither exactly for town or for the trail. He soon disappeared through the office door.

Cowboy eased the team up to the platform. "Sent to get a parcel shipped to John Dowling," he said as he handed the freight man paperwork given to him by the old man. He was rewarded with a small but particularly heavy wooden crate. It took all the efforts Cowboy and two railroad men could muster to heave the freight into the wagon. Stenciled to the top in bold black paint was the name "Plymouth Iron Windmill Company—Plymouth, Michigan."

Having thanked the depot men, Cowboy stood next to the wagon wiping sweat from his face with a huge red bandana. He thought for a moment how little help Dowling would be getting this box to the ground once he carried it back home. The consolation Cowboy hoped for was that Emma would cook another boggy top pie for supper. Dessert was not in his arrangement with Dowling, but Emma still snuck him a fresh cut of each new pastry.

The young owner of the grey pony nodded to Cowboy as he untied the horse's leathers. Cowboy nodded in return, but was really trying to decide whether he favored Emma's egg custard or her deep dish cinnamon apple concoction. He only needed to stop for her and her few purchases, and make the easy trek home in the squeaky buckboard.

It was not to be.

Cowboy marveled to watch a few events confluence to produce such incredible tumult. It took less than a single second.

First, the locomotive fireman pulled the lever to release the steam brake's hold on the front wheels. Escaping boiler pressure produced a hissing cloud that swirled in a rush onto the tracks. The accompanying heat was hot enough to make even the most ardent non-believer shout, 'there is a Hell'.

Second, the engineer tugged the chain, emitting an ear-splitting blast from the pudgy brass whistle. The reverberation, coming from so near, set Cowboy's teeth on edge.

Third and last, that combined cacophony might as well have been the starter's pistol beginning a horse race. The grey pony took six fast strides on a wild path directly away from the frightening racket.

The rider pulled the reins hard, one leather in each hand. He tried to stop the horse or at least slow him down. That didn't work. Instead, the pony began to crow hop, punctuated by erratic kicks of both hind legs. Unable to throw the rider from his back, the pony whirled back the way they'd come. He sprinted toward a narrow alleyway. Wooden signs, low-hanging beams, and cantilevers made passage on horseback questionable. The pony determined to use those obstacles, instead of a tree limb, to scrape the man off the saddle.

Cowboy stepped into their oncoming path, shrugging off his coat as he did so. That he threw over the horse's eyes and ears with his left arm. Then he jumped up to encircle the pony's neck with his right. Feet splayed, Cowboy dug his boot heels hard into the dirt. He inched fingers up the horse's mane until he could find the desired spot. Just behind the ears, near where neck bones meet the skull, nerve pathways bundle. With his thumb, Cowboy could feel it beneath the horsehide. He mashed with all his strength.

Immediately, it had the wanted effect. The pony began to slowly circle toward the direction of the thumb. He also began to bob his head up and down as though counting. Almost at once he went buck-kneed and wobbly; legs spreading until the chest nearly touched the ground.

"Get off," Cowboy shouted over his shoulder to the rider. "And stand clear."

The man needed no second instructive. He was to the dirt next to Cowboy before the pony drew another breath.

With the horse still blindfolded, and now disoriented, Cowboy threw a stirrup over the seat. He unbuckled the cinch and shoved the saddle off with the flat of his hand. The pony began to recover a bit. Cowboy grabbed the bridle's cheekpiece. "What'd you pay for this useless fuzztail?" he asked. "More than ten dollars, and you was hoodwinked."

"The fellow had a whole string of them," the man said. "Got him for five".

Hearing that, Cowboy loosed the throat latch behind the horse's jaw. He jerked his coat clear of the pony's face and slid the bridle off. Freed once more, the horse scallyhood away, fast enough to beat the Dutch. He ran to the open country just north of the depot.

Cowboy shook the dust from his coat before putting it back on. "I'm John Calvin Quinn," the young man said. He stuck his hand out. "But folks most call me Cal. I owe you much thanks, mister." His voice had the edge of tremor in it. Cowboy shook and nodded, but said nothing. He noticed that the man's grip quivered ever so slightly. No other outward sign of the man's brush with certain harm evidenced itself in his manner.

Uncomfortable with the silence, Cal then asked, "What do they call you?"

This direct lack of manners brought a near-smile from Cowboy. "Call me the one who knows horse flesh a lot better than you do." Without being asked, he put the man's saddle and bridle into the back of his wagon, next to the freight box. "Reckon you'll be needing another goose-rumped colt now that your pony's gone. Let me carry you to the livery other side of town." He bent to pick up a stick from the ground. With it, he began to scrape the caked dirt from the bottom of his boots. "I noticed that pony was fierce nervous when I brought the team up to the depot. Didn't like being tied to that post, with all that city clamor around him." Cowboy tossed the muddy stick back where he found it.

"What makes a horse that way? Cal asked.

"He had that look," Cowboy said. "Best I figure, he was a lightning-spooked horse. Most are kilt when the bolt strikes. Some are singed bad, others burnt something awful. Ones like yours just stay skittish all their lives." He nodded to himself as well as Cal, "Better off in the wild."

They both stood. Cal looked around this unfamiliar locale. "I'm not a man to pull a cork, or I'd buy you a drink," he said. "When I want to refresh myself, or steady my spirit, I use one of these." From his vest pocket he withdrew a small fold of paper. He shook broken bits of a licorice into his palm, offering them first to Cowboy then selecting a big piece for himself. "Soothes the nerves."

Cowboy took the candy, but pocketed it for later on. He climbed onto the buckboard, motioning for Cal to join him. "What brings you to Cowtown?" he asked Cal.

"You're not quite a Cheechawko, but I expect you ain't been here long."

"If by that you mean newcomer, then yes. I'm here in support of the family business. We're building a feed lot off the new railroad spur just this side of Leesville." He pointed with an extended arm to a spot true north.

"That land must have cost you dear, if'n you bought it off the railroad. Those boys ain't cheap," Cowboy said.

"And you'd be exactly right, except my grandfather owned a substantial interest in the Michigan Central line until recently Vanderbilt bought him out. The spur and the land was part of that deal," Cal said without sounding the braggard. "And before you ask, my father, along with McCormick and Lawry, ran the stockyard owned by grandfather's railroad in Chicago. He's in Nebraska now establishing a similar but larger operation. So I get this outpost as a chance to prove myself, which is great because I love this country."

Cowboy assessed the man again with this news in mind. Although young, he appeared confident if not also capable. And he sure-fire didn't panic when the little pony spooked on him. "Ain't seen it yet, but sounds like you got your work cut out," he said.

"Oh my yes," Cal blurt out with a laugh. "I have four flat cars stacked with newly milled lumber and posts from northern Minnesota just sitting on my rail siding to be unloaded. The surveyor and his people are busy from sun up to sundown staking the land out for the livestock pens. And, the labor foreman I hired three months ago in Calumet showed up two weeks late." Cal laughed a bit longer this time. "He's only now putting together a local crew." Cal's look darkened. "I only came here today looking for my trunk with all the business papers and books I've needed since the beginning. It was onboard with me when I left Chicago, but got offloaded in St. Louis somehow. They're having a devil of a time getting it the rest of the way."

"Some fellers couldn't track a steer through a bunk house," Cowboy said. "But like as not, they'll find it for you. Soon I hope." The wagon and team was just approaching the first of the mercantile buildings. Shadows were beginning to show on the sides of those structures as the sun made its way further west.

"What I really need is another set of hands," Cal said. "I need someone really good at organization and that can work well with numbers. They should like handling lots of detail and be used to dealing with strong personalities. They ought to be from around here and know the local ways." He turned to Cowboy with a half-serious look. "Above all, they need to maintain a pleasant demeanor always. Especially with me."

"Guess they'll need to turn up the wick, too, when time comes." They both laughed.

"Yes," Cal said. "That goes without saying." He seemed baffled. "I've talked with several possible folks, but found them all lacking. I doubt some could tell a housecat from a skunk." His face lightened. "It's a good position, though. They could grow with the corporation, become indispensable."

Cowboy continued to listen, but began to search the wooden walkways with his eyes.

"I suppose that I've just described some personage living on the likes of Mount Olympus or in the halls of Valhalla." Cal said. "Nevertheless, you seem like a man would who'd be a good judge of character. Anyone come to mind?"

At that moment Cowboy spotted Emma. She sat on a bench in the shade of a store's overhang. In her lap was

Cowboy's hardback Bible, next to her a small pile of bags and boxes, full of the items she'd come to town for. So concentrated was she on her reading, Emma did not look up to see the wagon approach with her tall new friend and the accompanying stranger.

Cowboy swiveled on the seat to give the man his best straight-faced serious look. The slight twinkle in his eyes flashing there did not belie that effort. "Now that I think on it, Cal," he said. "I just might."

* * *

At first, Dusty only tolerated the petting and scruffing by the friendly young woman. Emma worked her hand up the long neck to the ears. Then Dusty actually leaned his shoulder towards her like some big cat pointing out a favorite place to scratch. "I think he's partial to you," Cowboy said as he heaved himself off the front porch stoop to stand next to the girl. He'd been admiring her new duds as she attended to his horse. Stout stoga boots with thick soles, ready-made canvas trousers that hung loosely on her frame, and a pullover three-buttoned shirt with its long woolen tails tucked in. A wide hat shaped into a low crown - the kind favored by wagoneers, hunters on the prairie, and Buffalo Bill Cody himself - sat atop her head.

"Cal said we'd be working outside most of the time and I'd need clothes like these," Emma offered in response to his knowing grin.

"Suits you," Cowboy admitted. He gazed back at the porch to see her few possessions stacked there: a carpet bag stuffed with clothing and a small box holding trinkets and collectibles. From that box Emma took

Cowboy's leather-bound Bible. "I couldn't go without returning this." He took it with just a nod. "I read in there how important giving your word is." She said. "God kept His promise by sending His son into this world. Because of that we are all saved if we believe in Him." Cowboy smiled at both her words and the earnestness showing in her face. "Can't say as I fully understand all that I read, but I intend to keep studying it." Emma looked as happy as Cowboy had seen her. "I'll get my own Scriptures out of wages, once I pay back the advance," she said. "Spent most of that on this outfit and renting the back room at Old Miss Hagebak's house over in Leesville."

"Needn't bother," Cowboy told her. He opened the saddlebag on Dusty's hip. From that he took a small parcel wrapped in butcher paper and twine. Emma opened it, surprised to see it was a new Bible. "Last time in town, I came across the Salvation Army man down on the main street. For a few coins tossed on his drum, he was glad to part with it. He had a passel of 'em. Guess he figures Cowtown is full of sinners."

Emma blurted, "Oh, thank you." And before Cowboy could prepare himself, she jumped in with unexpected speed to throw her arms tight around his waist, burying her face in his chest. He could feel the strength of her bear hug. If not a bear, then at least a grateful cub.

"Don't get to fussin' now," Cowboy said in words barely audible. He could feel the redness flash his cheek and earlobes. "I ain't done nothing special."

Releasing her grip only with sheer reluctance, Emma studied the big man. "Oh no?" she said. "In less than the matter of one week you've managed to set right all the promises broken to me in three years. That's more than nothing."

"Did that how, exactly?" he asked.

Ticking them off with her fingers, Emma recounted, "First, my time of service at this house is finally over. Lydia found another girl to do the cleaning and such. And they're actually paying her a little something." She touched her second finger. "A complete stranger has treated me with the dignity and caring one shows to his close family. I never felt that before." She touched the last finger. "Because of you, a young man is coming this morning with his buggy. When he leaves here, he'll be taking me with him to another town." Cowboy followed her outstretched hand to where she pointed. He turned to see Cal headed toward them, pulled by a magnificent bay mare.

"I'm leaving too," Cowboy said. "Got the wood stacked and the chores done. Now's time for me and Dusty to be setting out. Got to see if I can find this other pard from my buckaroo days. Should be on the way to where I'm heading."

"Give me a promise of your own making," she asked at last. "Say that you will come see me again, when your travels are through."

Cowboy took his hat off. "I give my word," he said solemnly. Then he smiled. "It's no secret. Only way back to Texas is along that trail," He pointed. "And through this town. I'll be back." Then he grinned enough to show teeth. "I expect that by the time me and Dusty come through, you'll be Cal's querida."

"What's that?" she asked matching his merriment.

"South of the river it's how we call a gal our sweetheart. He's a good man, I'll let y'all work that out." Cowboy turned to mount his ride, but Emma pulled him back by the elbow. Standing on tiptoes she kissed his cheek. Tears welled in her eyes. Cowboy's too. "Adios, chica," he told her in farewell.

With a handshake and a word of best wishes to Cal as he stepped from the buggy, Cowboy took the saddle. They made the short distance to the trail, turning north. "She's in good hands, Dusty," the big man said. He urged the buckskin to a trot.

Cowboy and Dusty loped the trail together at an easy pace.

Their journey had begun.

A Word Given
Study Questions

1. Emma had been betrayed by those closest to her, including her parents, her aunt and uncle, and finally by Billy Mitchell. Have you ever been lied to or taken advantage of in a similar way? How did you deal with this betrayal?

2. Cowboy told Emma that "a word given is a promise kept." What do you suppose causes people to go back on their word and not keep their promises or take advantage of others?

3. Can you think of a time when you haven't lived up to this motto yourself? If so, what caused you to act in such a way? Is there any way to go back and fix things now?

4. In the story, Emma reads in the Bible that God kept His promise by sending His son into the world with the offer of salvation for any who would believe in Him. What does the fact that God kept His word reveal about God's character? Does this make you more likely to believe that God will keep his other promises that are found in Scripture?

Talking Rock

The west can hide a man. For bandits on the dodge or some puncher just looking to get lonesome, open land begets miles and miles of solitude.

Cowboy's pal, Frankie Peppers, had no price on his head - this time. There was no reward poster calling for his arrest or capture, and no one had put a bounty on him either - not even under his real name. When old Uncle Chacho determined it was no lawman he was talking to, the old man let slip where Peppers might be hiding out.

It took Cowboy three days riding Dusty hard, forty miles over rough ground to find where Frankie had last been spotted. A week more and he rode up to an isolated trading post to find Frankie deep in the building's shadow, sitting on a broken Montgomery Ward box. Cowboy's friend held thin rolling paper in one small hand. He shook tobacco shreds loose from a Bull Durham pouch with the other. Frankie took his time thoughtfully constructing his next precious smoke.

Cowboy could not see Frankie's eyes beneath his very wide vaquero's *chapulla* he wore flat atop his head, but there was no mistaking that familiar pointy chin. The straw hat, with its knotted rope for a hatband, came from south of the border. It was what the people there called the "shade-maker."

Striking a match against the wall, the little man drew in a lungful of breath. He tilted his head back as he did so, stopping when his eyes looked into those of the tall rider seated atop the beautiful buckskin. "Dang it, but you ain't Frankie Peppers," Cowboy said in disgust. "You sure as blazes got to be close of kin."

It took the balance of the afternoon, and the gentle inducement of hot tortillas, spicy carne, and beans cooked by the little *mamacita* in the back of the store, to get Frankie's half-brother to open up. But once fed, the man proved to be quite the talker. "Goes on just like Frankie did", Cowboy laughed to himself.

The man finally shoved the empty plate away from him, wiping his mouth on the back of a sleeve. "Ain't hiding," he said. "Not now. The fuss last summer over that man's cattle amounted to all but nothing. Sheriff didn't like it much, but he had to let Frankie go. None of them cows had any brand on 'em at all." The brother took his time poking between two back teeth with the nail of a little finger. Inspecting it, he seemed genuinely disappointed to find nothing further to eat. "This time of year Frankie and some other *vaquero* ride out to the flatlands on the other side of that mesa." He nodded at the small window in the wall beside them. Cowboy turned to see a long escarpment in the distance, blood red in color as the sun's rays struck there. He judged it to be most of a good day's ride, if not more.

"Can you say more precise the place I'd find him?" Cowboy asked.

In response the man stood. "Well," he said. Searching the store, he walked to the cook stove to select a piece of burnt remnant from the ash pile. On the way back, he took up a gray scrap of muslin he found on the floor. "You follow the creek out yonder - don't know the real name. 'Round here we call it the Salakoa - 'till you get to the river, then head west." He began to draw a map on the cloth with the thin sliver of charcoal. "There's a shallows about halfway along the mesa, an easy place to cross. Doubt the water will even come up to your stirrups this late in the season." He looked up from his crude cartography, concerned with the detail but satisfied. "Even a fiddle-foot could track the path of broken sage and chaparral Frankie made getting to the tall grass. He's not trying to hide nothing, just looking for horses. Sells them to the Army." The man handed Cowboy the drawing. He judged the big stranger could get there from where he sat, but he was careful not to ask why he seemed so determined to go.

* * *

Cowboy dipped the canteen back into the narrow stream until the bubbles disappeared. He squatted. His backside pressed against the incline of one creek bank, a leg outstretched. His boot mashed against rocks on the opposite slope. The water meandered into a shallow curve just beyond him. It turned away from the mesa without a river in sight. Should he follow the creek or head toward where he thought the tallgrass actually was?

Before he could puzzle that out, Cowboy needed to let Dusty drink too. It might be some time before they came to sweet water again. He didn't know this land, and he was about to ride away from the only true source of it he could see. Taking off his broad hat, weathered but still

35

rain tight, Cowboy flipped it downside up. With both hands he scooped it into the stream until it filled. Then using all the skill of a P.T. Barnum circus acrobat, he whirled his belly against the steep bank and rested elbows on the level ground. Dusty drank all that was offered from this hatful, and another, and most of the third.

Cowboy clambered up next to his horse, waving the hat back and forth beside his knee to air it out as he considered their state of affairs. "You know, Dusty, at a time like this Mama would snatch me up by the shirt collar and stare into my eyes. She'd fuss I was lost as an Easter Egg." He laughed as he strapped the canteen back to the saddle. "*Estas perdido.* That's never a good thing." Cowboy looked back the way they had come. He could no longer see the timbers of the trading post roof. "Way I figure it," he said to the back of Dusty's twitching ears. "We ain't lost exactly. We're just riding lands we never crossed before."

Cowboy used the remaining sunlight and half the next day's to bring him to the mouth of the bench at the bottom of the mesa. From where he reined Dusty in, he could spot the grassland in the distance. Before that lay a maze of short canyons; most with sheer walls. For a long moment Cowboy considered the various passageways, until he selected one he judged afforded the most direct path.

Entering that first canyon, Cowboy craned his neck to gaze up the steep sides. Both were red as autumn sunset. Light refracted off quartz and feldspar scattered along seams and ledges. The air carried the whiff of something Cowboy could not ignore, but did not recognize. He did, however, detect two sets of horse prints in the loose sediment of the trail winding crookedly before him. They looked no more than a week old. "Frankie," he said, guessing; glad that none were yet returning in his direction. With the sun no longer straight overhead and hidden by high walls, Cowboy and Dusty rode in the bright diffusion of alpenglow, comfortably passing through the unfamiliar, yet enchanting, landscape.

Cowboy eased Dusty around a dog leg's bend toward the west. He expected to find the canyon widen into its exit there. Instead, he found himself staring across a small alluvial flat, an almost perfect circle some fifty feet edge-to-edge. A mass of monolithic sandstone loomed upward, to a great height, at one edge of this clearing. The now unobstructed sun flooded the wall with radiant light. Cowboy sat motionless staring at what he saw twenty yards in front of him. Wonderment gripped his features.

He stepped down from Dusty with practiced ease, and led the horse by the reins to the middle of this formation. Close to the wall, a series of log-sized volcanic tuffs shaped into slags lay where they'd fallen from the mesa top. Cowboy stared up to fully examine the wall's uneven surface. It shocked him indeed that what he'd seen at a distance could be the same as he was looking at now. It was not the mirage he'd first imagined.

Ancient peoples inhabiting this region in past times obviously had selected this one spot as a holy place, Cowboy reasoned. He'd heard such campfire talk and rumor, but this was the first he'd come upon.

The bright patina of the red coloring carried a consistent hue the length and breadth of the wall. Along its surface, in groups and arcs and clusters, sizable figures appeared. Austere stick men stood next to wild animals. Concentric symbols surrounded unidentifiable markings. And, a series of arrows pointed a jagged pathway through the entire menagerie. Each appeared in bright relief to the wall's otherwise burnished color.

Cowboy slid off a rawhide glove, reaching over his head to touch the outline of the closest figure. His fingertips ran along the figure's edge for a ways, then along the rough red wall surface, and back to the figure once more. It became obvious to him that the men, animals, and symbols had not been painted on the rock as he first believed – but had, in fact, been scratched into the wall with some crude implement. The artistic gouging, he reasoned, had revealed the somewhat orangey-yellow layer underneath. How a rock could come to have two colors, Cowboy could not fathom.

While he struggled with this bafflement, he heard Dusty blow a double snort through wide nostrils followed by the beginnings of a whiny deep in the throat. It muffled out almost inaudible. Cowboy knew these to be the sounds Dusty made only when the big horse grew uncomfortable. And, that horse feared little.

Cowboy flinched, more amazed than startled to see two Arapahoe standing not six feet from him, each eyeing him with silent caution. Except for Dusty's warning, he'd not heard their approach. The old man looked at the same time both brittle and resilient. His thin frame could not be hidden by the billowing hand woven shirt. White hair covered his ears before draping over the shoulder. Thin leather gathered the locks together to resemble a pony's tail.

The other seemed no more than a child of three or four. His dark hair was matched by the even blacker eyes. He carefully kept the elder between himself and the tall stranger.

"*Tay kosh kutay?*" the old man asked in a series of guttural rumbles. He jabbed the index and middle finger of one hand in front of him, first at Cowboy then the wall. When he got no firm answer, he asked again. "*Tay kosh kutay enwende?*"

Cowboy raised both palms upward, shaking his head and giving a slight shrug of the shoulder. "I don't speak your tongue, grandfather. *Habla español?*" Neither language drew a response from the old man beyond a patient stare.

The man studied Cowboy with an unguarded curiosity that bordered on scrutiny. He saw the wrangler's knife at his hip, but noted also that no pistol hung there. After another moment's silence, he nodded once to Cowboy and turned away. The old man and boy walked without a sound to a knee-high slag that faced the sandstone. Taking up a cross-legged position on the rock, the old man raised his eyes to the sky. He began to recite a lengthy litany that continued as his eyes then affixed the wall in a blank stare.

Without warning, the man sprang to his feet and took a position close to the markings. He focused first on a thin line that curved into an almost complete loop before encircling itself again and again like some never ending whirlpool. He moved quickly next to a fantastical shaped human figure, much larger than any of the many stickmen that dotted the wall. These he pointed to as they clustered closely at one spot, only to diverge into scattered bands headed toward various compass points. For long minutes, in his deep foreign tongue, the old man called out words that to Cowboy, seemed to describe these various peoples. A flurry of pointed arrows, broken lances, and upside-down men and horses dominated the center of the wall, which brought a somber tone to the man's recitation. But as he stood just beneath the small figure of what looked like a big horn sheep pierced by three arrows, he touched this figure with his finger tips and began to wail without control. In the silence that followed, the old man stepped over to the series of intricate geometric shapes at the wall's end. He began to chant once more, one hand on the wall, the other touching just above his temple.

At last he sat next to the boy once more. Long minutes of silence followed. At intervals he would turn to the boy, whispering or speaking in low tones, he would impart some private information to the youngster.

A smile came to Cowboy's lips. "You don't need bother with them hushed tones," he said to himself more than to the Arapahoe. "I don't *sabe* any of it." He'd found his own slag to sit upon, near where Dusty fed on what sparse vegetation the horse could find thereabouts.

One hour became two as Cowboy watched the Arapahoe. Both sat without word or much movement. The old man, eyes closed, appeared in a trance. At regular intervals his head would nod a half-inch as though he were either agreeing with himself or counting off some unseen list in his head. The boy, for his part, alternated his attention between his grandfather, the wall, and the ground in front of him. It amazed Cowboy that a child so young could remain so still. Most he'd seen that age spent all their time in rambunctiousness or unfettered caterwauling.

It amazed Cowboy further that this wall captivated him so. The etchings touched a certain curiosity at the back of his mind and began plaintive stirrings in his heart. What he did not understand but could only feel, was a tug at the bottom of his soul. He confided as much to the buckskin, "It's like I've hidden something deep down inside, Dusty. A long time ago. But now I'm hankering to know the answer to questions I can't even put into words yet. It's a bafflement." The big horse bobbed his head as though he understood.

Cowboy studied the wall's figures and symbols once more. He made no further understanding as to what it all meant, but he could reckon this collection held some great message. Obviously, it did for the two Arapahoe.

His thoughts were interrupted by the sound of a horse's footfalls coming his way. Frankie Peppers stopped the pony near Cowboy's mount and slid himself quietly to the ground. He slapped Dusty on the rump and smiled.

"I thought that was you, *mi hermano*. No one rides a horse like this. Big. Sure-footed. A *Boyo Coyoté* with black stockings. Saw you through the spyglass when you came through that flat bench between the mesas. Couldn't help it. Storm clouds in the sky behind you. Made the *cayuse* stand out like blooms on prickly pear."

Cowboy smiled at his pal. He remembered how listening to Frankie's clipped staccato could wear him out. Lassoing with a stiff rope would be easier. At least the riata would get softer over time.

The little man pumped Cowboy's hand a dozen times while eyeing the old friend with some concern. "Don't see no star. You ain't law. I'm always careful who's law and who's not. No bounty hunter, I think. Too early for elk. Not enough of you to be chasing down mustangs." Frankie paused at last. "Why you here, amigo?"

Before Cowboy could answer, Frankie turned his head to stare at the two Arapahoe. He knew many of their tribe thereabouts, this close he might recognize one of them. He did.

"*Mira!*" Frankie hissed out in a slow breath.

Close-set dark eyes grew big as nickels. "White Raven himself," he whispered. "*El Borcado* of the entire Three

Fires Clan. The Dream Seeker. Named him for a bird they saw the day he was born. Has the gift of vision no man - red, brown, or white - can match." Frankie turned his head back to face Cowboy. His voice still hushed in reverent tones. "The old man squats there on that Talking Rock. The one he's huddled on with the boy. Stares at this wall until his mind can see a blazing pathway. It's said he gains the power of that image. This assures the tribe's success." The little man nodded once toward the old Arapahoe, in awe. "That's big medicine."

Without waiting for Cowboy to respond, Frankie grabbed the horn of his saddle with both hands and swung himself up. "*Vamonos, amigo.* I'm not superstitious, but I don't need no hexes either." He turned his horse back the way he'd come.

Cowboy threw a leg over Dusty at the same time. Leaning hard, and with an outstretched hand, the wrangler grabbed his friend by the elbow. "Before you light out of here with that pony's tail on fire, tell me what you know about them etchings," Cowboy said. "I can figure some." He indicated the whirlpool. "And I can suppose at others." His hand swept up to the mid-wall, but stopped as he pointed. "What I want to know is why the old man cried hot tears when he put his hand on that sheep symbol. The one with all them arrows in it."

Frankie shot a hard look at Cowboy. His hurry to leave drained the color from his face. He said, "My mother's people all are Three Fires. But she took up with a Spanish *vaquero, mi padre*. We lived near the villages. I came here as a young boy to learn the stories. The people were happy once, but soon the clans took separate ways. Battles broke out between them. War to the death." Frankie was careful to look neither at the wall or White Raven, only at Cowboy. "With so much fighting, clans could not grow crops or hunt. People starved." He leaned his head back as if to better recall his teachings. "The Three Fires sent twelve young men and boys to hunt for game. Only one came back alive, carrying that big horn struck with many arrows. It was called the Dark Time." Cowboy could see the distant sadness float across his friend's face. "Meat from that big sheep kept them alive until the peace that soon followed."

Frankie spurred his horse hard, then yanked it to a stop. A thin wicked smile crossed his lips. "My father's people tell it different. The old *viejos* say Three Fires hunters," Frankie scrunched his dark face into a wrinkling of unconcealed scorn. "Not so good, eh? Very bad." He shrugged. "Why else would it take three arrows to slay one sheep? The only one they ever managed to kill, so they HAD to honor it on the wall." Frankie grinned. "Maybe old White Raven was crying for their lack of skill." He burst out with a loud guffaw, showing very white and very straight teeth." It did not, however, draw the attention of either Arapahoe.

"Now that's more like the Frankie Peppers I rode the trails with," Cowboy drawled through a grin of his own. "I wondered how long you'd gab before the talk turned to food. Seems I recollect, with all we had to learn about horses and cattle, the only thing you ever wanted to know was when we'd eat."

"Maybe," Frankie said. He let the mocking grin relax into something close to impishness. "But eating's important, you know. Especially to a skinny *vatto* like me."

"I see you still can't stop a horse without jerking the reins." Cowboy said. "Surprised that apron-faced hoss didn't throw you, like some of them others did." He laughed. "How far's your camp?"

"An hour maybe," Frankie said. "If we hurry, we can get there before sundown." He tapped a saddle bag with the leather braided strap tethered to his wrist. "I got some tequila. *Poquito*, not much, but enough for tonight. We talk old times, eh?" The vaquero waited for Cowboy to ease Dusty along side his pony. "Speaking of eating," Frankie said. "Raphael is boiling some prairie chickens and sweet grass tubers into a stew for supper. He spices them with sage bush shavings and bits of brickle weed." A pink tongue shot out to lick part of his upper lip. "*Andale, muchaco!* Time to eat!"

Before another word could be said, Frankie quirted his pony hard across the flank, jolting him into a sprint toward the mouth of the canyon. Frankie leaned forward in the saddle, almost to the nag's bobbing neck, to brace himself against the pony's lengthening stride.

Dusty needed no encouragement. In an instant, he was at full gallop hot on the pony's heels as they raced headlong toward the open prairie. Over his shoulder, Cowboy took one last glance at the wall, watching etchings disappear in a bouncing blur.

* * *

The gust from a morning wind blew ash and hot sparks from the campfire into a swirl. Cowboy and Frankie both moved where the smoke would be out of their eyes. Each held a tin of strong coffee, barely touched.

"Ray's dead? *Dios mio*," Frankie said. He made the sign of the cross quickly, kissing the back of his thumb's knuckle at the last. He glanced at the sky above him, then shook his head in disbelief. "Ray always took good care of me. Used to call me 'Franito'. I yell at him 'I'm no thumb-sucking *niño.*' He starts calling me 'Little *Franito*' after that just to gnaw at me." Frankie pointed a thin finger at Cowboy. "He'd always buy drinks when I had no money. And, he'd finish fights I got into with those loudmouth drovers in those trail town cantinas. *Caramba,* now he's dead."

"Yessir," Cowboy smiled, recalling his friend and mentor. "The man could surely raise hell and put a chunk under it."

Frankie sat stunned in silence. Cowboy let the man have his quiet. Raphael busied himself with morning chores elsewhere, so the two had the fire to themselves.

The vaquero roused himself once more, smiling this time."Ray always could charm the *bonitas*. The ladies loved him. And he gave me this spyglass, I don't remember why." From his range coat, Frankie pulled out a small brass telescope, once used on a Navy frigate but won by Ray with three queens and a pair of eights. Frankie stared at it now as if it were a lump of gold.

With a gloved hand, Cowboy took the pot off hot coals. He poured some in Frankie's cup, then into his own. "Ray was a good pard," he said.

"*Si,*" Frankie replied. "Selling mustangs to the Army was his idea. Decent pay and more nights sleeping under the stars. Thought it would never end, but then he changed. At a campfire just like this. Not eight-ten miles north of here. Just the other side of Round Pond."

"The itinerant preacher man, that big fella?" Cowboy asked.

"Big as you, *hermano*. Maybe bigger." Frankie said. "Hands like a grizzly paw, voice louder than a cornered buffalo. Soft grey eyes that looked into yours, and knew all your secrets." He stared down at the coffee getting cold in his hand. "Said his name was Vandenaker or something like that, but just to call him Brother Van. He scared me. Ray took a shine to him. They talked all night. Next day preacher was gone. Ray was different."

"How's that?" Cowboy asked.

"We gathered up what little ponies we had and took them to the quartermaster. Got our money and headed south to Cowtown. He courted Esmerelda, went to church meetings regular, gave up drinking and fighting, and bought the boarding house with that little stable." Frankie smiled at the memory. "He married Essie and settled down to become a good citizen. His woman could sure cook, but I came back up here anyway."

"Last time I was to visit them," Cowboy said. "Ray told me his soul felt free as any mustangs galloping open prairie. He knew something I still don't know." Cowboy tossed coffee dregs on dying coals. "I came up from Texas to find just what that was, and it seems the trail has led to this Brother Van. Any idea as to his whereabouts?"

"Way he talked," Frankie said. "He liked to winter with the tribes near what those people call 'the trembling earth'. South of the Yellowstone basin." His eyes narrowed. "You think of going up there? It's a long way, amigo."

"Maybe if I knew where," Cowboy replied. "You any better at map-makin' than your kin back at the trading post?" I don't want no antigoglin path this time."

"Agh!" Frankie said. "Hildalgo's a *cabrone*." He shook his head in rapid sweeps. "You don't need no map. See that snow peak on the horizon?" He pointed to a white speck barely to be seen in the distance surrounded by deep blue sky. "Follow the water to that mountain. I hear the river starts below this rocky waterfall at one end of a high meadow. This Brother Van described his lodge squeezed along the other side." He looked at the mountain once more and counted on his fingers. "You got time to get there and back before first snows. Not by much."

"Tight," Cowboy said with more caution than certainty. "But doable. I reckon I'll chance it."

"Why ask for trouble?" Frankie asked. "There's things in the woods up there that can eat you. And the horse too." Frankie spread his palms out wide. "Does this have something to do with that look you had when I rode up in the canyon? When you were watching those two from the tribe."

"It wasn't them, it was the etchings." Cowboy said. "That was a pretty big wall. I knew what was up there had meaning, but I couldn't make sense of it. A song with verses missing." Cowboy pulled the leather bound book from his coat. "It reminded me so much of the first time I took up the Scriptures out on the trail. The more pages I read, the more muddled it became. No matter how powerful I knew the words to be." He put the book away. "I couldn't do it by myself. My brother Marcus helped me some, my father too. I was hoping Ray could give me some guidance like he always did for me on the trail."

Cowboy stood to put his tin cup back in the saddle bag. He began to adjust Dusty's cinch. In a moment more, he turned back to Frankie. "Shared a bunkhouse with this fella from England. Smart hombre, mucho schooling. We called him the Professor. Said something I'll never forget, so I made him write it down. "

From the inside pocket of his coat Cowboy removed a rumpled paper. "Frenchman named Pascal studied numbers. He thought a lot about a man's mind. And heart, too. He said this." Cowboy read from the script in his hand. "'There is a God shaped vacuum in the heart of every man which cannot be filled by any created thing, but only by God, the Creator, made known through Jesus.'"

He returned the paper to its hiding place. "I got that exact emptiness, Frankie," Cowboy said. I ain't a man who goes barkin' at a knot, so if it takes trekking to that mountain to help me find Jesus, so be it."

Cowboy gazed at the snow peak for a moment. He stuck out his hand for Frankie to shake. "Best of luck with the ponies, *compadre*. I'll look for you on my way home."

"I only see good things in your travels," Frankie said at last. *Viya con Dios, hermano*."

Cowboy turned Dusty toward the worn track that ran along the river's edge.

They loped the trail together at an easy pace. Their journey had begun.

Talking Rock
Study Questions

1. In the story, Cowboy sits for hours studying the etchings that have been carved on the canyon walls. He doesn't know what they mean, but he knows that they're important. He likens them to "a song with verses missing." Have you ever shared a similar experience? Describe what you felt in that moment as you tried to comprehend the incomprehensible.

2. Cowboy is on a quest. His friend Ray had discovered something that had radically changed his life. Cowboy saw a peaceful freedom in his old friend, and he recognizes that he still doesn't understand exactly what that change was. It's kind of like the etchings on the canyon wall. On a surface level, Cowboy knows that his friend found Jesus, but again, this knowledge is like "a song with verses missing." Cowboy is missing something. Can you relate to Cowboy's deep hunger to understand these spiritual truths?

3. Cowboy describes an emptiness in his soul. He reads the quote from Pascal that "there is a God shaped vacuum in the heart of every man," and

he acknowledges that he needs to fill this void. Do you agree with Pascal and Cowboy? Are all men and women created with this innate need for God?

4. Do you sense this vacuum in your own soul? At a deep level, do you feel like you are incomplete without the life of God living inside you? If so, do you understand how to fill that void, or is the Bible still an undecipherable etching that you can't understand? Would you be willing to reach out to somebody else to help you understand what Scripture says about our need for God?

Somedays

"Beauty can fool any man, even if he's mindful."

Cowboy heard his father's words rumble through his head again as plainly as if the old man were standing right beside him. "Sweet smells tempt him," the parson droned on. "But unexpected touches of the hand surely make his heart go giddy-up. And, whispered promises cloud the otherwise most even judgment." He thumped the Good Book in front of him, concluding: "There's danger when distraction addles a mind away from steadfast thinking."

Riding through the lodge pole pines, Cowboy recalled that confusing lecture, or whatever it was, when the Gospel Man gathered his boys in their tiny Atascosa kitchen. His father truly believed the day drew near when their bubbling adolescence might compromise proper treatment of those few females close of age living thereabouts.

No concern for the fairer sex back home made Cowboy reminisce that awkward evening. Instead the thought came triggered by Frankie's warning, not one week past, about those things living in the woods through which he now traveled.

Cowboy could not help but marvel at what he saw, and smelled, about him. Across the plains of Texas where he'd wrangled cattle years on end, a tree'd be thought "tall" if it grew as high as Dusty's ears. This army of evergreens he gazed at stretched overhead more than ten times his own height. Each tree spanned the width of a broad man's shoulders. Its leaves like substantial mending needles, but emerald green in hue.

Cowboy drew a needed deep breath in this thinning air. The strong scent permeating the thicket carried a heady tang to Cowboy's nostrils. It brought sweet metallic taste to his tongue.

Giving himself a hard shake in the saddle, Cowboy threw off the dreamy daze that had begun to grab hold of him. This brought him back to his usual keen awareness. In caution, he slid the rifle halfway out the scabbard and back in again, wanting the Remington ready should he need it at the haste.

The act of touching that weapon reminded Cowboy that should he not find Brother Van in the next day or so, he'd need to stalk some game for food. Or, he'd be reduced to eating *pinyon* nuts from the many pinecones strewn along the way. He might even have to chance trapping one of those red-backed Chicaree – what the folks out this way call their chattering shade-tail squirrels.

"Sun's full up," Cowboy told Dusty. "But don't seem to make it to ground betwixt these tall trees. Breeze become a wind now, and makes the air a might coolish this high up the mountain." He rolled the range coat's collar tight against his neck, wrapping his bandana round it just to keep the chill off his skin.

Reining Dusty to a stop, Cowboy pondered their changing situation. The trail they'd ridden ended, edging a wide-spread deep ravine. The slope bottomed at a gushing, fast-moving stream. That, in turn, emptied into the river the two had followed since the mesa. Scattered boulders clinging to both embankments evidenced sizeable rock slides in the region, but none recent.

For a moment, Cowboy chewed on the notion that it would be next door to a miracle just to ride Dusty safely down this incline, let alone cross that flood. Even if he managed that he figured, they'd need a stroke of luck to heave themselves up the steep bank on the opposite side. "A risk not worth taking," he nodded to himself. Another go-across somewhere upstream would need the finding. Just the same, he took the time to stare through trees beyond this noisy gorge, seeing piney woods give way to an undersized but sunlit clearing. Cowboy reckoned this likely not the preacher's meadow, but it might be holding an elk or two.

Hopeful then about the prospect of fresh backstrap and tenderloins for supper, Cowboy turned his horse away from the river. He nudged the buckskin into a slow walk, letting Dusty pick his way, sure-footed, among the many rocks now scattered on the meager path. For long minutes Cowboy rode chest bent to saddle horn, studying the dirt in the path that ran nearly parallel to the creek. Others had passed this way ahead them. Some weeks before, judging by the impressions he saw. The hoof prints there in the mud came from a barefooted pony, and not one Indian-shod either. Various animal tracks mixed in with them as well. That made the first sign he'd seen of another rider since he left the tallgrass flatlands. It could be a mountain man, or perhaps the preacher himself. Cowboy hoped it might portend well.

Topping the rise, Cowboy could see the water below him actually jetted through a rock-strewn hollow in the hillside some quarter-mile up the way. This formed a natural span above the stream. It seemed the traveler's path would cross there too.

Along the track in front of him lay several outcroppings of weathered granite. Each extended out far enough to force the trail around it on its way toward the arching bridge. It amazed Cowboy that these craggy formations evidenced so much tremendous upheaval. Great slabs of rock leaned hard against adjacent slabs of rock. Occasionally, narrow gaps occurred between, none wider than could barely hold a man. Dens perhaps, for the smallest of wildlife.

Cold wind gusts coming from the river freshened at Cowboy's back. This caused unruly hair to flail against his cheeks and brow. He tugged his big hat further down and guided Dusty around that first tall ledge.

Squinting now at that stretch between them and the bridge, Cowboy realized that Frankie's premonition had come to pass.

* * *

Standing flat on two hind paws, a bear fattened by a summer full of eating leaned forward to grab a slender tree trunk in its sizeable claws. He held the grip just about at chin level. His big head canted all the way sideways right. With its mouth now full open, the bear managed to get its jaws around the entire tree. Slobbering, it scraped the bark back and forth with long incisors. This left both markings and scent for all creatures coming along this path to find, especially any other bears that might also occupy this stretch of mountain.

The bear froze in place. For a moment, no sound could be heard except the air sucked in and panted out of its protruding nose. It had caught the scent of something new. Abandoning the tree, it stood erect. The head jerked over a rounded shoulder in the direction of that smell. The bear's dark eyes narrowed on the sight of horse and rider. It seemed to consider whether these two were predator or prey.

Dusty saw the creature a split-second before Cowboy did. They did not react to it the same. The wrangler lurched over to grab his weapon at that same moment when Dusty staggered a violent half-step sideways, beginning the turnabout back the way they'd come. This jumble of confused movements landed Cowboy hard on the ground with a thump. His horse – and the still sheathed rifle – now raced away at the full gallop.

That left just Cowboy and the bear. The cowman knew defending himself against this considerable beast with only the knife on his belt would be the sheer act of a fool. For once, he followed his mama's often repeated advice. He walked away from a fight. For about two steps, then he ran.

The bear, for his part, thundered out a terrifying bellow that Cowboy wagered could be heard in the next valley over. The animal dropped to all fours, head swaying side-to-side. For one guarded moment, it watched Dusty run off in a noisy clip-clop. It took another quick sniff at the wind. Then this corpulent predator concentrated its complete attention on Cowboy; smaller, slower, and fumbling now in a panicked retreat. In an explosion of speed not seemingly possible by a creature of its unwieldy size, the bear tore after the fleeing human.

Cowboy knew from campfire talk that a bear could match the fastest pony in a foot race, even up to a country mile. He stood no chance at running. The rock formation afforded his only possible hope. Grasping a handhold just over his head, Cowboy tried to pull himself up to begin an uncertain climb, but his boots could get no firm purchase on the flat granite surface.

He didn't need to turn to know how close the bear was getting. Cowboy could hear the breathy grunt expelled each time that hairy monster's front paws landed. The bear sprang off again almost at once. By then, the hind paws had caught up in this series of quickening running leaps. With the beast now almost on him, Cowboy abandoned the second attempt to climb the ledge at that spot. He scurried toward another where the rocks looked more likely to give him his ascent. He did not get there.

Unexpected, but providentially provided, the big man slid sideways into a narrow crevice between two rock slabs. Although not wide, the cleft extended from the muddy ground where Cowboy stood to the outcropping's uneven crest. The gap narrowed as it reached upward but never fully closed out the dimming sunlight. Its cramped opening could not accommodate the width of Cowboy's weathered Stetson. The hat scraped off and fell to the base of the opening. No sooner than his John B. hit the ground, a big paw swatted it away.

The protective cranny provided scant space to accommodate the big man. With the back of his head rubbing the granite behind him, Cowboy could turn his head almost without his nose touching the rock wall in front of him. His range coat and vest added enough extra bulk that Cowboy could feel the walls press his chest and back. And although the cleft ran six to seven feet deep, a flat rock's protrusion stopped Cowboy about halfway back. Catching him just at the hip, this rock, the size of a dinner plate, looked no thicker than his little finger. It did not, however, budge when Cowboy pressed a palm down on it using all his strength. He needed to squeeze back further, away from the opening, before the bear figured out that it could likely reach Cowboy with a long foreleg extended.

The snout came in first, poking barely into the opening. The bear sniffed a bit, clacking teeth together as it did so. Cowboy then watched with great revulsion as the jaws jacked open again. The bear let go an unnatural sound, less a roar and more a screech of pain. It unnerved the wrangler that he heard it to be the cry of frustration. Cowboy knew it signaled the great beast's obsession to snag him, no matter how long or what effort it eventually took. The cave filled with the stench carried by the bear's breath. That reeked of carrion and rotted gooseberries. Cowboy had never smelled the like.

Next, the big head turned sideways so that one angry eye glared at the human. Cowboy found it fitting the ear he could now see was missing a chunk of the top half. The jagged remains indicated a bite mark. The bear took time to look up and down both walls of the cleft. It stared at the topside opening for a long moment as well. Cowboy guessed the bear was searching for some other way in. Tentatively, it pawed hard at each side of the opening, but nothing gave way.

Cowboy's breathing came faster now. His attempts to break the rock plate continued to fail. Even though he knew it was coming, he still jerked when the bear whirled around to scrunch his shoulder into the breach. A searching paw, flailing claws extended, thrust at his knee caps. One large claw swiped across the toe of the boot. That left two deep scratches. That claw, blunted from continuous digging in the dirt and ripping at tree bark, split almost a third of the way up. A second swipe caught the hem of Cowboy's jeans. That removed a small tattering of cloth.

Cowboy leaned as far back as he could. He managed to avoid the next few swipes, so the bear withdrew that paw. In its place, the animal maneuvered to switch legs. In that few seconds lull, Cowboy whispered a prayer. "Lord, please help me," he said. "Don't let it end like this. I come a long way to find answers from that preacher man." The second paw probed the crevice with movements more awkward than the first. "I can't do this by myself," Cowboy went on. "I see now that I never could."

In this new posture, the bear seemed not to be able to reach in as far. Claws barely, but clearly, missed the boot with each swipe. So again, the animal readjusted, going back the original and more successful position with the other foreleg.

Cowboy felt his breathing relax. A cautious stillness seeped into his consciousness. Using just the heel of his palm at the exposed end of the protruding rock plate, he lifted up on tiptoes to bring his full weight and muscle to bore down on it. Long seconds he strained against it, ignoring the bear completely. First a muffled cracking sound, then a loud snap as the rock tumbled to the ground. In two-and-a-half sidesteps Cowboy was to the back of the crevice, out of the bear's reach. Looking at the broken rock at his feet with unbelieving eyes, Cowboy said, "This grateful sinner thanks You for that, Lord, with a humble heart." He eased out a long sigh. To restore himself further, Cowboy let his body go limp against the wall, his cheekbone pressing flat against the rock. "I won't let Your act of kindness, to help me here, go to waste."

***

The remainder of the morning blurred into a series of swiping paws, threatening growls, clacking teeth, snorts, sniffs, and hateful looks as the bear continued to hound his cornered prey. Cowboy wondered how long the bear's resolve would last, and what he himself would do exactly once the predator was gone.

Cowboy didn't have to wonder long. With his head looking away from the opening, it took him a moment to realize that all noise had stopped. He turned to see the entrance unencumbered of fearsome beast. Figuring it some trick to draw him into the open, the wrangler stayed right where he stood but strained to hear all sounds for some foretelling clue.

Without the animal blocking his view now, Cowboy could look out and see a tiny part of the meadow and most of the bridge that crossed the rushing stream. Two hours passed. In the distance, through that narrow opening, Cowboy watched a bear amble across the crest of the span. It made its way to the meadow, rolls of fat rippling with every step. Even that far away, Cowboy could see the gotched-ear. His tormentor had moved on.

Standing so long in such a crooked position left Cowboy somewhat stiff. Stretching helped, but what the cowman really wanted was the comfort of finding Dusty. He curled lower lip against teeth, sticking his tongue behind and let out a whistle. Loud, long, high-pitched, and shrill. He waited, but nothing. Cowboy turned to watch the bear one last time. He saw the brute turn east at entering the meadow, away from the trail.

Again he whistled, and this time in the distance Cowboy heard Dusty's muted whinny. The third whistle brought the big horse trotting up to Cowboy's side.

"It's good to see you, you old hoss." He said to himself as much as the horse. For a long moment he petted Dusty. That seemed to reassure the animal a bit, but gave him greater comfort. At the same time, Cowboy checked the horse for signs wounds or injury. That whole while he stood where he could still keep an eye on the bridge and the meadow, and all that space in between.

Grabbing the reins, Cowboy swung up into the saddle he thought he'd never ride again. As he considered the wisdom of pushing up the trail knowing the bear had gone nearly that same way, his thoughts were interrupted by the sounds of a tremendous commotion. Coming from a spot in the meadow blocked by the tree line and in the direction where the bear had turned, a familiar roar echoed across the gorge. It came in waves, one of anger, one of ferocity, each growing in intensity.

Cowboy suspected that the bear finally found the prey he hungered for, but that unlike him, this one put up something of a fight. Before long all the clamor stopped and the mid-mountain peace returned.

He gave the brute time enough to gorge himself. Cowboy figured a well-fed bear was a slow-moving bear. He planned to cling to the trees at the meadow's edge, skirting in the opposite direction along the trail. He pulled the rifle from its sheath, nonetheless, to hold as he rode. He would not be empty-handed again if he faced that bear a second time.

With this plan in mind, Cowboy rode Dusty across the bridge and into the clearing. At first, he did not believe what he saw there. Stopping at a distance, seeing no movement, Cowboy eased Dusty closer. The horse did not spook on him this time. Dusty sensed no danger in that big heap lying there in the meadow grass.

Cowboy stepped down. Rifle in hand, he moved to the carcass. "*What in tarnation?*" he said, still not believing. At his feet the gotch-eared bear lay dead.

"Doggone, that's not the fate I woulda expect of you. And sure as blazes not today." Cowboy scanned the space between every tree that edged the meadow. Anything that could have done this would be an even bigger monster. A greater threat to him and Dusty, but Cowboy saw nothing of the like. Only the competing sounds of jays and chattering squirrels could be heard filling the grassy clearing.

He squat on his boots to take a closer look at the bloody dead body of the beast that had tormented him so. It lay twisted on its belly; one shoulder to the ground, the other jacked at an odd angle towards the sky. The skull looked brutally crushed. One eye clung to the socket only by a small flap of skin. Twin puncture wounds, six inches apart, perforated the snout in several places.

Cowboy touched the broken head. He considered for a moment the massive force needed to inflict this much damage. He could understand the shredded throat and the scratches on the neck. What he could not fathom was the huge chunk of flesh missing from the dead bear's rump. About twice the size of Cowboy's fists balled together, tooth marks showed this hunk of meat had been bitten off. "Dang," he said. "That's plain mean."

A quick scan of the trees again, and Cowboy shoved the rifle back in the leather sheath. He turned back to the bear one last time. "If I was to ponder all this out," he told the heap of fur and bones. "I'd say we both got schooled some today. And it was all about arrogance." He looked down to see the claw with the long split pressed partly in the soft ground. "You thought you was the meanest thing in the valley. Carried on always surly and disagreeable, like some bushwacker raised on sour milk. Then you met the one that done you in. Another more vicious than you."

Cowboy touched the split claw with his finger, feeling the roughness of its surface. "My own self? My arrogance grew from all that I learned as a cowman, the skills I developed, and the trust I have – or had – in myself. A day in the cave took all that out of me." He poked now at the ribs and spine with the heel of his hand. "Ray once told me, 'It's not so much over-estimating yourself that'll get you in trouble. It's underestimating the other things around you.' Your failing was to pick on the wrong opponent. Shoulda run. Mine was to think I was boss in charge, and not admitting God is running the outfit."

Cowboy stood. "My brother Marcus often reminds me that Scripture foretells God will humble the proud and vanquish the ruthless." He studied the cut on his boot. "Today I know that to be true."

Cowboy mounted Dusty, thought better of it, then climbed back down. A grave look clouded the wrangler's eyes. "Some days," was all he said. He tried, but failed, to put a weak smile on his lips. "Some days a fella's more grateful than glad." Cowboy reached inside the coat to draw the knife from his belt. An hour later Cowboy took the saddle again, leading Dusty to the far side of the meadow.

They loped the trail together at an easy pace. Their journey had begun.

Somedays
Study Questions

1. Cowboy learned a thing or two that morning in the cave. First and foremost, he realized that despite all of his training and experience, he was never really in control of his life. Just one wrong turn on his path showed him that life can change in an instant. How about you? Are you trusting in your experience, intelligence and training to get you down your own path? Or do you understand that there is a higher purpose that helps guide all of us?

2. Stuck in the cave, with the bear swiping at his legs and trying to devour him, Cowboy whispers a prayer: "Lord, please help me." Can you relate to this experience? Have you ever called out to God in the midst of a crisis, acknowledging that He is ultimately in control? Did God respond, like he did for Cowboy?

3. Cowboy quotes a verse from Scripture, found in 1 John 4:4: "Greater is He who is in you than he who is in the world." Through his close call with the bear, Cowboy finally understood that he's not the boss, but that God is running the outfit. Have

you come to that realization yet, in your own life? And if so, what assurance does this Scripture verse bring to your own experience?

4. At the end of his ordeal, Cowboy musters these words: "Some days a fella's more grateful than glad." Can you relate to this? Do you have a grateful attitude for all of the blessings that you've experienced in your own life?

Bison's Dilemma

"I come a long way to find this man, Dusty. I just never expected to find him nekkid." He laughed those words out as he looked down between the horse's ears from that small bluff overlooking the waterfall.

Cowboy shuddered at the sight. Not from seeing the pale wet skin, but the knowing that the high mountain river Brother Van bathed in flowed ice-cold. A surprisingly-wide, cascading torrent crashed the rocks below with unabated roar. This formed a large catch pool, filled with swirls and eddies. Narrowing, it became the river once again. Somewhat of a light rolling mist clung to the water's surface. "Ain't exactly headwaters," Cowboy said to his mount. "But might as well be. It's as far as we're going."

He eased the big horse down a winding path, around the last of a thick pine grove, and into the open. The meadow appeared even bigger than Cowboy remembered Frankie's sketchy depiction being. His saddle pal got most of the detail right. The waterfall verged the west end of this huge high-mountain pasture, and a small cabin snugged the hillside at the tree line to the east. It took Cowboy all of several minutes to trot Dusty the distance to the riverbank.

As the wrangler approached this solitary figure, the man shook more water from his bushy hair and continued buttoning his faded union suit. Frankie's description came fairly close; the girth and height was nearly that of Cowboy. The man watched the horse and rider with an open expression, unguarded eyes, and a passive smile. At no time in Cowboy's approach did the man show any unease, much less alarm.

"Howdy," Cowboy said as he reined Dusty to a stop. "Ain't you a mite chilly standing there in just your long johns? I reckon that water's got to be more than a tad coolish this time of year."

"Truly," the man said. "The Yassahanna is not known for its warmth." He gazed at some ripples near the shore. "Instead, our river is celebrated for its great mystic quality."

"How's that?" Cowboy asked, caught up with curiosity.

The man responded with a toothy grin, "The native people say that any person that touches it can only utter the truth thereafter."

He looked up at the rider for a long moment of silence. At last he said, "Tall cowboy, riding a big buckskin with a white star on the face, broad-brimmed Stetson, and a stout mustache." He narrowed his stare, looking into the other's face. "I can't see your eyes underneath that hat of yours, but I'll wager that they're blue or grey. Tilt your head back a bit." Cowboy did so. "Indeed," the man went on. "Just what I said. A pale grey-blue. That makes you Ray Patterson's friend." The man stood motionless as he waited for Cowboy to acknowledge that obvious fact.

Astonishment flashed Cowboy's features as the wrangler struggled with the notion that he'd just ridden a thousand miles to find this stranger he hoped was Brother Van, only to hear that the man already knew him. Or at least the man knew whatever Ray had told him.

"I'm Brother Van," the man said. "I expect Ray spoke some about me, too." With a casualness borne of a peaceful confidence, he slid boots over bare feet. Next, he donned a thick woven-wool coat with very large hand-made buttons. The man walked through the ankle-high meadow grass to stand almost touching Dusty's shoulder. Raising a massive hand, he gave Cowboy's a firm shake.

"You look tuckered from your travels," Brother Van said. The preacher himself did not. His entire countenance beamed a formidable energy. "Let's head back to the cabin," he continued. "And I'll feed you a decent meal. Then I'll share with you how, intended or not, the timing of your arrival is fitting. Happenstance, I believe, but you certainly have cut it close."

Cowboy wheeled Dusty back around while Brother Van mounted his own horse, a silver-dappled dark-brown pony. Its tail and mane flowed pure flaxen. The wrangler noticed at once, as they trotted across the meadow together, the preacher's horse struck ground with a single-footed gait. It obviously was bred to handle the steeps and falls of the mountain trails.

Cowboy noticed as well that Brother Van kept eyeing the big bundle tied behind Dusty's saddle, but the man said not a word until they reached the tiny pine-log structure butted against the small hill. Once inside, Cowboy saw the cabin held more room than he would have thought. The front wall with its single door entrance and the two sides were stacked pine. But what should have been the back wall opened into a cave-like hollow that quickly tapered into the narrows of an old mine entrance.

"It gives me more space than I need, but a pleasant retreat to cool off in when the summers get too heated," Brother Van said following Cowboy's big-eyed gaze into the tunnel. "Go ahead and settle your horse while I get the fire started. I can fix us up some fresh partridge; just brought down this morning; some beans, and day-old sourdough with a little black lick to sop it in."

That brought a smile to the wrangler's face and almost a rumble to his belly as he tended to Dusty. He placed the bedroll with its tarp and soogans on the ground, and the saddle next to it, but the big bundle he lugged into the cabin. "My ma taught us to never go empty-handed whenever we come to be a guest, especially if we was to ask a favor." Cowboy said. "I thought you might could use this up here in snow country." He undid the leather thong and unrolled the furry hide with the toe of his boot. Taking the bulging muslin cloth packed in the center, Cowboy pulled back a corner to reveal the choice meat he'd cut from the dead bear's carcass after he'd skinned him just the day before. "You can add this to your skillet," he said.

Brother Van bent to take the bearskin between his fingertips. He rubbed the fur with gentle strokes, occasionally tugging at the long hairs, and finally he sniffed the skin of the underside. "This is quite fresh," he said. "Did you trade for it?" The preacher looked up at Cowboy. "Or did you kill it yourself?" He then hefted the skin in both hands over his head as high as he could stretch. Another foot-and-forty-inches and Brother Van might have lifted it all off the cabin floor. The top of the preacher's gray head almost reached that of Cowboy's. But unlike the wrangler, the man's chest barreled like a pine's trunk.

"I done neither," Cowboy replied. "Me and what was this bear spent most of the daylight yesterday, him trying to claw me out of the hole I was hiding in, me squeezin' to make myself smaller." He raised up his right boot, pointing to the scratch. "That's him," he said. "And this is what done it." Cowboy pulled a thick, curved claw from his vest pocket. It held the deep split stretching a third of the way up from the blunted tip. Fresh saw cuts marked the jagged other end. "After a fashion, the beast got tired of coming up empty and just sauntered off," Cowboy continued. "By the time I gathered my horse back, the bear had walked over the ridge and out of sight. But when we rode up the trail to head your way, I come across his torn-up remains in this little meadow."

"A hole, you say?" Brother Van let his scruffy eyebrows furl almost together in curious disbelief.

"Yessir," Cowboy said. "He spooked my horse and I had to run for it afoot. Only the hand of God coulda led me to that narrow crevice in the rock wall. Saved me from certain dismemberment."

The preacher studied first the wrangler's boot and then his face long enough to assay the big man's worthiness. "Providential, most certainly," he said. His grave features relaxed into a smile. "Just like Moses, the Lord placed you in the cleft of the rock. A safe place for both of you, it turns out." In a voice much more bass than his generous body would indicate, the preacher burst out into loud but lovely song:

"He hideth my soul in the cleft of the rock,
That shadows a dry, thirsty land.

He hideth my life in the depths of his love,
  And covers me there with his hand,
  And covers me there with his hand."

A warm smile drew across Cowboy's lips. He did not know the words to that hymn, but for a moment he imagined his Daddy singing this very tune. He nodded his approval. "Wish I'd known that song yesterday. I'da shouted it at that bear to leave me alone," he said. Cowboy rolled the fur back up, tying the leather lash tight once again.

"I started to ride away from his remains," Cowboy nodded at the pelt. "But got myself back off Dusty. I wanted that broken claw as a reminder." He looked almost embarrassed to continue. "'Sides, I needed meat anyway. And figured his couldn't be any tougher than some of them storm-killed longhorns we'd eat pushing the herds up north. So, I skinned him." Cowboy touched the fur with the toe of his boot. "I brought you the hide. Might need another robe, or coat, or blanket for the winters this far north." He took a step back.

Brother Van eyed the ragged hole at the bear's rump. "That done by the beast that killed him?" he asked. Cowboy dipped his head "yes." The preacher held the gotched-ear skin between thumb and forefinger, "This looks bitten off," he said. "But these cuts are fresh. Yours?" Brother Van traced a finger over a series of alternating deep grooves along the ear's gnawed edge.

"They are for a fact," Cowboy grinned. "I notched him like a newborn calf, so anyone who can read the double over-bit earmark will know this critter belongs to the Bar Diamond D. That's the brand of the family ranch back down in Atascosa County."

The preacher said nothing, only giving the taller man the beginnings of a knowing grin. "I'm just grateful something else done him in, so I didn't have to tangle with him again," Cowboy said. "My tormentor one hour, laid low in the next."

"Indeed," Brother Van said, taking in the thought. "Thank you, son. You've given me more than you know." The preacher touched the skin once more; this time with a delighted admiration. "The local native tribes place great respect on the bear, his ferocity, and great strength. That gives this pelt big enchantment. They will see it this way: You were on a pilgrimage to see me when this bear attempted to prevent your journey. But through the power of your skills, you evaded the bear and outwitted him by staying just out of reach in those rocks. You even taunted him by letting him scratch only your boot." The preacher let the story carry him to even greater rhetoric. "As punishment for his misdeed of interference, the bear was killed on your behalf by an even bigger bear. Your journey here continued without further incident." Nodding, Brother Van waved his hand in Cowboy's direction. "That makes you a man of big medicine. That all this was done so you might meet up with me, I must therefore be big medicine, too."

Brother Van patted the skin with approval while Cowboy struggled to digest what had just been explained. "That's some yarn," the wrangler said, looking from the man to the pelt and back again.

"Yes," the preacher replied. "And I intend to tell it just that way, if not more embellished, to Manatah, chief of the Bend-in-the-River peoples with whom I spend the winter months. He'll receive it with great honor and we will become even greater friends." Brother Van raised himself to full height as his faced darkened in full concentration. He waited until their eyes met. "You didn't ride all the way up this mountain merely to hand over a bearskin, even a stately one. What's really on your mind?"

A simple enough question and the one Cowboy struggled with each long day in the saddle getting to this very meadow. "I saw the change Ray made in his life. He became a better man. He found the peace that came with his devout convictions. No matter that he was so wild in his past." Cowboy's eyes stared at the preacher but his gaze turned inward. "I have wrestled with myself, been of two minds, and come up short on how to find such contentment. No matter how much I read Scripture or how many sermons that I hear delivered; or even all the feeble prayers I've tried to say—that calm escapes me." Fatigue began to sap his strength.

"Any notion as to what keeps you from finding it?" Brother Van asked. "I can't imagine that with all Ray told me of his past that you kicked up any more sand than him."

The words caused Cowboy to suck up a quick breath. He let the air back out slow. "That's the nub of it, preacher. I did do worse. I pummeled this other fellow something vicious back home in Atascosa when I was little more than a youth. Broke him up bad." Cowboy shook his head with the dreaded memories. "Then I took to the cattle drives. Thought at first it was to spare my folks the upshot of all the mess, but I've come to know that mostly I was just running away from what I had done." Cowboy sank down on the only chair in the cabin. Brother Van watched him agonize there but said nothing, waiting for him to finish in his own time. "The boy's daddy owned the bank that held papers on our ranch," Cowboy all but whispered. "I knew for sure Ma and Pa would lose that and have to take up somewhere else. All because I had a stubborn streak, quick fists, and wouldn't back down to the likes of him." Cowboy's weariness grew more pronounced the longer he confessed. "I come a long way for your help."

Brother Van sat next to Cowboy, on the cot wedged against the timbers in the wall. He stared gravely at the sight of the torment gripping this man who'd traveled so far from home to rid himself of it. "Seems like forgiveness, or more precisely the lack of it, figures into what you just told me. But know this." The preacher took the Bible, which Cowboy had slipped from his coat pocket, out of the big man's grip. "I am not the answer. You'll find that here." He held up the small leather book before handing it back. Then he placed an extended finger on Cowboy's chest. "And with prayer, you'll find it here. Because of the cross, all your sins have already been pardoned."

Cowboy looked up from staring at his boots. "Pa's a man of the Gospel, and so's my brother Marcus. I've heard and read Scripture all my life. Even on the trail." He looked at the Bible in his hand. "Since I left home, whenever I read verse about the Lord's sacrifice and the grace folks were given I know it's talking about everyone else but me. What I done is too bad." His head went back down.

The preacher's quiet laugh broke the silence. He patted Cowboy's knee until the wrangler looked up again. "From what I've heard about you from your old pal Ray, and from what I can tell from your manner in this short while, you're a man who places great store in honesty." He seized Cowboy's Bible once more. "The Lord's forgiveness for all who believe is found in numerous Gospel verse; that's the written word of the Almighty himself. He has made us His promise."

The preacher smiled a knowing smile. "I can see that you're good-sized, from boots to brisket. But I don't think that even you are big enough to call God a liar."

Cowboy sat in continued silence, pulse evident at his temples, weariness bordering on defeat in his eyes. "Can't argue with that; sure enough," he said. "But what do I do now?" he asked.

Brother Van crossed his arms as he gathered the proper words for his answer. "I spend the winters far north of here, in a place where the ground trembles and ground water boils in shallow pools. The whiff of sulfur always clings to the air." He leaned forward to put his hands on his knees. "When the snows get deep, you'll find a bison or two huddled near that gurgling water just trying to keep warm. They won't freeze to death if they stay near the pools. But the problem is, there's no food to be found there. Nothing grows close to all that ancient sulfate. To feed themselves they must venture out in chest deep snow. Some ways away they'll stop to paw that snowfall to find the grass and vegetation buried underneath." He smiled with the knowledge of what he himself had seen. "I call that the Bison's Dilemma. Stay warm and starve or chance freezing but be fed."

Cowboy followed this tale of nature with obvious fascination. He could not, however, hide his underlying puzzlement. "That's a fact about those stumpy critters I did not know." he said. "How's that figure into Scripture or my own troubled situation?"

"The way I see it," Brother Van said. "Like the bison, you have a choice to make. Stay where you are in the familiar, somewhat comfortable state of your self-imposed unforgiveness, and starve yourself spiritually.

Or, you can venture from there, accept the Grace of God, and get your soul fed forever." The preacher spread his palms. "The decision is yours."

A glint of understanding began to flicker in Cowboy's eyes. He smiled.

"Let's get some supper going and follow that with a good night's rest," Brother Van said. "We both have a long day in front of us after sun up. I must leave for the tribes tomorrow if I intend to beat the first snows." The preacher's eyes revealed a growing fondness. "You found me just in time."

Cowboy still sat with elbows on knees, holding the Bible in both hands. The preacher placed both of his own atop the wrangler's. "You might want to read Acts 13:38-39 while I cook."

* * *

The morning sun had yet to peek above the ridgeline. Cowboy spent the most of two hours hustling to help Brother Van bundle the last of his portable goods and possessions from the cabin onto the pack animal's back and into the panniers. Looking at the heap of cargo lashed to the sawbucks, he reckoned the preacher subscribed to the notion, "Don't worry about the mule, load the saddle down."

"I do believe that, except for the last of the firewood and kindling, you got everything that was in there." Cowboy nodded to the tiny cabin.

"Not quite," Brother Van replied. "One last particular." He hurried off to retrieve it. In the minutes that passed, Cowboy did a quick tally of the entirety he'd seen the day before and of what he'd helped pack. He couldn't conjure up anything that they'd missed.

The preacher returned with a well-worn Big Fifty in one hand, and two stout pasteboard boxes in the other. Cowboy recognized the Sharps .50 caliber buffalo gun at once. He figured Brother Van kept it to hunt the elk on this mountain, but wondered why he kept it so hidden.

"I almost forgot that I had this," the preacher said. "I wanted you to take it." He offered up both hands to Cowboy. "Too big for my liking, but you might find it comes in handy if you face another bear on the trail going down the mountain." The man looked relieved when Cowboy took the rifle and ammunition from him.

"A man just don't give away one of his firearms like this," Cowboy insisted. "I couldn't let you go without."

"Tut-tut, young man," Brother Van said. "My .44 Henry will do me fine, and by-the-by it isn't mine. It originally belonged to a Franklin Horton. The late Mr. Horton foolishly left it leaning against a lodge pole pine thirty yards from where he scratched the rocks up near the pass looking for gold trace." The preacher shook his head at the thought. "The bear he encountered there made short work of him. Next to the Sharps, I found a lead rope tied to the tree with a halter still fastened to it; skin and hair left on the crownpiece. Apparently, the mule chose to lose a little flesh rather than suffer the same fate as Horton." The preacher's head shook again. "I didn't see that animal on that day nor have I since. I haven't heard it either. Goodness knows mules are not quiet animals, especially when they're lonely."

Cowboy agreed with a knowing nod, but looked at the rifle in his hand with some concern. Sensing that, as much as seeing it, the preacher offered, "I would not take such a weapon as this to the tribes. Even as a gift, it would only cause trouble. Before you rode up I figured that in the spring, I'd take it with me on the circuit and swap it for something at the trading post. Now I have a fine bearskin in its place."

At the mention of that word Brother Van's eyes widened in thought. "More than just a providential irony here, there's a lesson to be learned. Horton journeyed the mountain for gold, met the bear, and died. You journeyed the mountain for Christian enlightenment, met the bear, and lived. Your path was blessed, his was not."

Cowboy looked at the bear pelt tied to the packsaddle. That lesson, with all its paradox, would not be lost on him. He watched the preacher mount his horse and settle into the saddle. They shook hands with warmth, each wondering whether their paths would cross again in this lifetime. Brother Van spoke first. "The Lord forgave your sins and made the gift of salvation; never doubt that," he said. "Forgive yourself. What's done is done. Find this man you've wronged. Ask his forgiveness. Whether he does or not, you're righteous with the Almighty." Before Cowboy could reply, Brother Van nudged the dappled pony to a walk and led the pack horse into the meadow, headed north. Over his shoulder, the preacher shouted, "Remember, it will not be your gift until you accept it first." A brief wave of the hand gripping the reins, a nod of the head, and Brother Van fixed his attention on the trek to the winter tribal lands.

Cowboy watched him go until the man and horses were most the way across the meadow. He stowed the cartridge boxes in the saddle bag and lashed the big buffalo gun to his scabbard with strips of leather. Cowboy turned in time to see the preacher reach the bend in the trail as it disappeared into the tree line. His heart felt heavy – and at the same time very happy.

Cowboy twisted in almost a full circle so that he could survey the horizon in all directions. He studied what he could see of the sky. Unlike the plains, the other mountain tops surrounding him kept him from seeing at much distance; barely more than the blue expanse overhead. Brother Van had advised him not to delay his leaving. Big weather was headed their way. Cowboy could see no indication, but he trusted the preacher's caution.

"You know Dusty," he said. "When I was wedged in that cave being troubled by the bear, and you was off to parts unknown, I began to suspect that riding all this way was some fool's errand." Cowboy heaved himself in the saddle. "But the words that man spoke has made me think on my worries with a whole new mind." He smiled from the heart. "It helps to ease the spirit, and it sure-fire gives me *mucho que pensar*, a lot to ponder. But then, amigo, it's a long way back to Texas." Cowboy spurred the big horse.

They loped the trail together at an easy pace. Their journey had begun.

Bison's Dilemma
Study Questions

1. In this story, Cowboy tells Brother Van that he wrestles with himself in his mind, always coming short of peace and contentment. He knows what the Bible says, but he finds it difficult to accept those teachings. The Bible says in James 1:5-8 that a double-minded man is unstable in all his ways, driven and tossed by the wind and waves of life. Do you ever experience this sort of inner turmoil and conflict, like Cowboy?

2. Cowboy confessed to Brother Van that he has spent much of his life running from his past. Brother Van explains what Scripture says in Acts 13:38-39, that through the love of Jesus, God has forgiven all men of their sins and set them free in a way that the Law never could. Cowboy's sins were already forgiven; he simply needed to accept this truth and learn to forgive himself. Have you done anything in your life that seems too big to forgive? Can you accept the fact that this sin has already been forgiven by God, whether you choose to accept that forgiveness or

not? What might stop you from accepting this forgiveness and being set free from the weight of your sins?

3. Cowboy had a choice to make. He could stay in his familiar, self-imposed state of unforgiveness and starve spiritually, or he could step out in faith, accept the forgiveness that God had promised, and receive spiritual nourishment. Have you come to the point in your own path where you've had to make this same decision? If so, do you think that this is a one-time decision, or is it an ongoing state of mind to accept the forgiveness that God offers?

Never Seen His Face

A horse with an empty saddle wandering the trail alone, and no rider in sight, spells trouble. The man might have been pitched when his pony's foot found the gopher hole. Or possibly he tumbled when he leaned east at the time his hoss jack-knifed south. Likely the man got his spine wrinkled in the process. As a result, he lived out a cowboy's great fear: being left afoot. Injured, lame, stove-up, or worse; at the very least, the man ended up miles away from where he wanted to be. Now, shamefaced, he had to walk on thin-soled boots just to get back there.

Cowboy eyed the Claybank mare that stopped nibbling tall thread grass to eye him back. He sat saddle on Dusty, resting at a spot where the crest of the ridge they'd just topped opened on to an expanse of sage flats.

The land there held sparse collections of two-needle pinyons mixed in with juniper trees, copious amounts of black sage, and a sprinkling of Indian paintbrush. Undulating low hills with frequent exposed rock outcroppings stretched in almost a straight line to the south where the start of the plains met the edge of the mountains.

The mare's coloring looked a lighter shade of a red dun in the day's diffused lighting. Her feet showed four white stockings above the hooves, and a cob webbing of dark-ringed marks surrounded the cowlick swirl on the forehead. She carried a single-barreled pumpkin saddle on top of a thin gray blanket evidencing too much gap above the withers. Her plain headstall of the bridle attached to a short one-piece California reins. Something seldom seen this far east. Cowboy judged from the undersized saddle, the lone cinch, and impractical leathers, the rider must be a "show about." What old ranch hands out here call the dude wranglers. This rig was never meant for working cattle.

That thought of some green pea lost down along these mountain trails made Cowboy shake his head in sheer frustration. His quick scan of the surroundings did not uncover a single lost soul ambling off in any direction. Nor could he tell how long or from which direction the mare had been traveling. It puzzled him even more that no bedroll or saddle bags were joined to the mare's rump.

Before Cowboy could explore this unexpected circumstance further, he knew he'd need to take a closer look at the mare and rig. Pressing his left knee into Dusty's side, the buckskin eased two steps forward. The Claybank pricked both ears forward, aiming them at the big stallion approaching her. She let go a quiet whinny, but did not bolt or retreat. Cowboy saw alertness, not skittishness in her manner. Just the same, with movements of deliberate slowness he unstrapped the lariat from his saddle. At the same time he turned Dusty almost perpendicular to the mare so that the buckskin's body hid the coil of a fast loop Cowboy shook out with his free hand.

For minutes Cowboy, Dusty, and the mare stood motionless except for blinking and breathing. A fresh wind blustered in from the west. It blew occasional gusts ahead of the threatening purple clouds Cowboy could see racing their way from the horizon.

As the wrangler knew she would, the Claybank turned her head slightly away from the other two so she could eyeball some new distraction kicking up from that other direction. Cowboy swung one quick whirl at his side, then up over his head and releasing it in a single motion. The rope flattened, landing straight down over the mare's head almost at the same time she saw it coming. Cowboy almost never missed when he threw the hooley-ann. He spun the rope a turn or two around the saddle horn, but aside from a short head shake the mare never as much as flinched.

The occasional spattering of rain that splashed the sandy ground between irregular clumps of grasses came faster now. Each weighty drop pelting his exposed skin made itself felt - like Cowboy was being tapped with the stub end of a heavy rope. Pulling the slicker from the saddle behind him, the wrangler could see dense sheets of the darkening downpour headed his direction. A cold and wet soaking would make the ride back to Texas seem even that much longer. He wagered his oilcloth would be no match for the unfolding downpour. Brother Van had said it right about the storm.

To his left, at a distance of about seventy yards, a rock overhang jutted out almost touching a dead pinyon. Cowboy figured it to be wide and deep enough to shelter himself and the two horses from the encroaching deluge. He made one last scan of the basin for the owner of the Claybank mare he now pulled behind him by the rope.

His view now made smaller by the driving rainstorm close at hand.

A line of rock debris edged any entry into the overhang. Fallen from the ledge above, the stones varied from being larger than a wagon's wheel to looking no bigger than a blacksmith's box. Cowboy let Dusty pick the path through the rubble, and trusted that the mare would follow them without much fuss. Once out of the rain, the wrangler saw that this shelter was nothing more than thick strata of dense rock – one part providing the roof, the other forming a bare floor, narrow back wall, and a shallow partial side wall. The soil that had once been a layer wedged in between, now became an unexplained empty space. The broken top of the pinyon, gray and missing its bark, lay together with dozens of dried cones, collected splintered branches, and a jagged heaping of needles strewn along the rocky floor.

The rain continued to pound the prairie as Cowboy unsaddled Dusty and wrapped the woven leather hobble on each foreleg, between fetlock and knee. It was tight enough to keep the stallion from wandering, but loose enough to let him break free if there were real danger. The mare presented a different problem to the cowman. He did not have the second hobble. Although one could be twisted in a lariat quick enough.

Instead Cowboy looped the Claybank's reins over the stout end of the pinyon top. Before removing her saddle, he used the spread of his hand to measure the mare's face and jaw. Then he loosed the long rope from the mare's neck, unrolling it almost completely with an underhand throw. Cowboy doubled it back so he could gauge its span. He used half the length to tie a series of double overhand knots the way he'd been taught on the trail. Frankie called these quick fastenings blood knots, but

Ray preferred to dub them barrel loops. In a quarter hour and two adjustments later, Cowboy finished with his new sagebrush hackamore. Now the mare wouldn't have to fight the bit all night. Neither would she merely mosey away.

There had not been the time to graze the animals before taking shelter, and now twenty feet separated them from the closest grass. Even if some horses preferred standing in a steady rain, Cowboy decided to let them feed after first light. He busied himself packing some apple-sized stones into a rough circle near one wall where it formed a rough corner. That he filled with a mound of old cones hollowed out and stuffed with handsful of dry needles Cowboy scooped from the floor. This pile he covered with broken limbs, snapping longer ones to fit inside the rocks. Lighting the kindling with a match from his vest pocket, he soon had a proper fire going.

Cowboy huddled near the flames, listening to the rain slacken and torrent up again as he waited with practiced patience for the rocks to crackle. Then they would radiate heat as well. Warmth already began to bounce back to him off the rock wall. Cowboy knew that he had not the energy to make coffee. He believed it would be sufficient to just gnaw on the sourdough Brother Van had given him and chew on some smoked meat the man also supplied.

First though, Cowboy wanted to dwell a moment on thoughts the preacher had discussed with him. The wrangler also felt the need to read a bit of Scripture before he drowsied off into inattention.

He took the leather-bound book from the coat and placed it next to his knee. For a brief moment, Cowboy leaned back to let the wall support him. He felt shoulders start to slump. The lower back muscles began to relax next. A moment more and the rigors of the long ride jumbled against the turmoil of Cowboy grasping Brother Van's unvarnished guidance. These competing needs fell together ever-so-slow, like some campfire ladle stirring an iron pot of thick stew. The wrangler closed his eyes without thinking. He stopped fighting it, and in a moment more gave in to the slumber.

* * *

As though poked with a burning stick, Cowboy bolted upright where he sat on the uneven rock floor. The fire still blazed inside the now blackened circle of rocks. It threw off great light. Even in that clear brightness, Cowboy knew he dreamed what now stood before him. A man; bearded, generous face, and eyes that held his own as though tethered. It was those eyes, although composed and gentle, that pierced right into Cowboy's heart. Past that, they looked down into the core of his soul. The wrangler realized he looked into the face of Christ Jesus himself.

Cowboy heard those first words spoken. They came to him in a clear sound, despite the steady rain. He jolted once more, when he realized their meaning. "You know my name," Cowboy said.

"I know all of my Father's children," came the soft reply. "You are my brother, for we are both sons of God." The eyes now embraced Cowboy with an earnestness the wrangler could almost touch. Those eyes gazed a moment at Dusty dozing alongside the mare before turning back to the wrangler wedged against the jagged wall. "Hear this," the voice said. "I have already paid the price; your sins are forgiven. Fear you not." His lean hand swept until it indicated the ponies. "You have journeyed far," the clear voice said again. "But now you must travel back, as the prodigal returns to the home he once left." An approving smile formed on slender lips. "Tell them all what I have done for you this night."

Before Cowboy could form the words to speak again, he felt exhaustion engulf him once more. With a hand still clutching the Bible, he fell into a bottomless, transforming, and now dreamless sleep.

* * *

It surprised Cowboy not one bit that the sun hung a foot or more above the far horizon. He woke to the clumsy sounds of the big buckskin blowing repeatedly and stomping his hooves with some impatience. "I swear, Dusty," Cowboy told his horse. "You're noisier than a painted cat when you ain't been fed. Or are you just in a lather to hotfoot it down the trail; me straight-legging all the way and shaking hands with grandma, too?" Cowboy laughed as he moved to stand. He shook off the dirt he'd gathered during the night, placed the book thoughtfully back in his coat, and turned his attention to the ponies.

Foregoing his usual meager breakfast makings, Cowboy pitched the saddle on the Claybank, cinching it only loosely. He left the halter secured to her jaw, but tied the all-but-useless fancy bridle to the saddle's horn. He knew, even with his back turned and without seeing, that Dusty watched all this with big dark eyes assessing his each movement. "Your turn, big fella," Cowboy said. For a moment he stroked the withers and rump. He checked as he did every morning for signs of anything that needed tending before unhobbling the legs and tacking up.

"You was there last night when the dream come on me," Cowboy said. He removed the bit before sliding the bridle on so Dusty could graze and still be held by the reins. "It was some powerful, what I saw. Clear as anything," he confided, putting on the woven blanket and the saddle. "Like the bewildered folks in Scripture, the Lord spoke to me - not no one else. Jesus spoke just to me." Cowboy stood without moving. He held the cinch's end in his hand, yet to be tightened and buckled. "I never seen his face before that moment. Drawings in church and the Good Book aplenty, but never his actual face." Dusty relaxed twitching ears. He stuck his head back a bit, jutting out the jaw, as if to agree.

Cowboy led the pair from under the overhang, reins in one hand, halter's rope in the other. He stopped at a spot where the thread grass bunched together in large clusters. While Dusty and the mare devoured thick green shoots easily pulled from the soggy soil, Cowboy made his way to the top of the hill that gave way to the overhang at its north point.

As he chewed on the vittles he'd set aside for last night's supper, the wrangler turned in a slow circle. His eyes stopped at any tree, shrub, rock, or shadow that might be hiding an injured man. None held his attention for long.

At each point of the compass, Cowboy let out a loud, "Hell-lew." That got him nothing; not so much as an echo in this open flatland. Satisfied after a second turnabout that he done what little he could to find the missing rider, he made his way back to the almost-fed horses. Cowboy indulged them another quarter-hour, then fixed Dusty's bit and pulled himself into the saddle.

He intended to reach the grassland's edge by nightfall. If not by sundown, then by next day's afternoon.

* * *

It troubled Cowboy that for the full three days since leaving the rocky overhang he had kept the river in sight off to his right, but he had yet to pass all the way through the sage plateau. "I don't rightly recall these ragged brush and juniper lands being so extended," he told Dusty. "But if I was to say it true, most ways from leaving Frankie's camp my mind was full and my heart was overflowing." He patted the horse with his reins hand, the woven lead being held in the other. "Good thing you can follow a trail by your lonesome." He turned around part way to look at the Claybank that followed quietly at the end of the long rope. She had occupied his thoughts a great deal since they found her. The wrangler knew pulling her like this all the way to Texas would involve more work than just riding Dusty. Since he had yet to sit saddle on her, Cowboy could not judge the mare's worth as a mount. "Maybe I'll give you to Emma as a surprise," he told the mare. "Or maybe I'll sell you and that fancy rig first town I come to has money." The mare gave no reaction to his words the way the buckskin usually did. She merely looked off in the distance while he talked. Cowboy just shook his head at this lack of manners. To his way of thinking, this horse was not uneasy near people. But neither did she much cotton to them either. She responded to all his directions by rote, like some horse-haired machine. He'd yet to see the tiniest spark of spirit displayed in anything she did. "Leading a red-hided ghost back to Atascosa ain't my first idea of something needs doin'," he told the Claybank before facing back around.

The sun had arced its way almost to overhead, now free of clouds that covered most of the morning's skies. The brightness coming with it caused Cowboy to squint as he scanned the sage looking for what he remembered to be a stout juniper thicket, no broader than thirty-feet. A single twin-needle pine stood apart by half that distance. It towered above the loamy ground. In between, the trail began its descent down into the rolling grasslands.

In the glare, he could not see any trees grouped in that fashion. Tugging down the Stetson's brim, Cowboy shaded his face enough for him to see without slitting eyes. What he gained in shade, he lost in vision. The hat blocked what was to be seen then at the distance. Grabbing the Stetson's crown and pulling it loose, Cowboy held it at extended arms-length. It blocked the sun once more, but he now saw the horizon. There, in the distance he picked out a thicket located near a lone tree. The pine seemed shorter than he recalled. He would know soon enough. On the way up-trail, Cowboy notched it with his knife. The trail mark would confirm he traveled the right path.

Less than two hours later Dusty, Cowboy, and the mare started down the trail's narrow decline. Before them, stretching from horizon east to that of horizon west, an unending set of gentle hills rose and fell. The continuous grass undulated, blown by a west wind. "Yippee-yai, Dusty," Cowboy yelled with pent-up enthusiasm borne of relief. "That's the prairie that stretches all the way back to Amarillo." His grin did not stretch from one ear to the other, but neither did it miss by much.

Ahead of them on the trail, Cowboy saw the same puzzlement that had intrigued him weeks before. For reasons not obvious to the wrangler, a lesser trail spur angled off to the grassland in a steep and rock-strewn path. Cowboy followed the route of this pathway with narrowed eyes. He soon realized that near where the path met the grass, a herd of twenty or so grazing *mesteño* ponies stood watching him. The mustangs looked every bit the feral strays the Spaniards name them for: high necks, sloping shoulders, narrow muzzles, and low-set tails. Their colorings ranged from black to bay, chestnut to pinto, and variations typical of their kind. What could not be missed was the prominent black stallion that walked to place himself between the ponies and Cowboy. Chest full out and neck arched, this dominant male of the herd looked at the two horses on the hillside, not the wrangler. The stallion whinnied long and high-pitched. Dusty replied only by pointing both ears in the herd's direction. The mare whinnied back, moving up beside Cowboy as she did so. The Claybank apparently wanted an unobstructed view. Cowboy could see the beginnings of excitement flicker in her eyes. "Well now," he said in tones of understanding. "It's a genuine stud hoss that gets the life in to you."

Cowboy climbed down, pulling the slack out of the mare's lead rope. He stepped closer to the Claybank to better judge her reaction. From over her shoulder he gazed more fully at the prancing stallion. His coat glistened, unmarked by any other color. The black stretched from nose to tail. Given its ample size, Cowboy guessed it to be out of true Irish draught horse stock. How such an animal as this came to be here on these

Great Plains seemed a mystery to him. But the stallion loomed big enough to dominate any contest for mares in the herd. Cowboy delighted that Dusty showed no interest in besting him.

Without warning, the mare nickered a mournful call. Cowboy could feel the tug against the rope in his hand. The wrangler made a quick decision. He tossed a stirrup over the seat. In seconds he had the mare's cinch undone. The saddle fell to the rocks in the path in a thump. A moment more and the halter slid over her ears and off the jaw. He raised an arm above his head so as to quirt the Claybank on the rump with the rope. He stopped. If the mare was to go, the choice must be hers alone.

She gave Cowboy not so much as a final look. The mare stumbled, with focused determination, down the rocky path. She stopped a good ten feet from where the stallion trotted out to greet her. They eyed each other for long seconds before the bigger horse stepped up, neck arched, flared nostrils an inch from hers. For more than a minute they both inhaled each other's breath. Satisfied that he knew her smell, the stallion turned to rejoin the gathered mustangs. Carefully, the stud kept himself between the herd and this new stranger.

The stallion gave a signal that Cowboy did not see, and at this distance could not hear. In a rush, the herd bolted headlong toward the west. The Claybank trailed not far behind. Before the stampede crossed the small rise, Cowboy caught one last glimpse of the Claybank's face. He swore he saw her smiling.

Having stepped himself down the lesser trail a pace or two, Cowboy turned back to find himself eyeball to eyeball with the buckskin. "Is there a name for that look?" he asked Dusty. "'Cuz I already know what you're thinking." He looked to see the trampled grass the mustangs left behind. He wondered how long the herd would take to include the Claybank. Looking at Dusty again, he said, "I'm just a cowpuncher raised down in Texas, but even I can calculate this out." He held up an index finger for the horse to see. "First, Brother Van ministers to me at the cabin." He raised the second finger. "Next, I have the dream where Jesus speaks to me." He raised the third. "And just now, the Claybank rejoins her own kind so she can run the prairie the rest of her days on the mustang's journey." Bemusement wrinkled into a weak smile. "I know it's time to go. Not just to Texas, but back home to family in Atascosa." He shook his head as his eyes focused on nothing. "It's been too long and I'm tired of running."

From the range coat pocket, Cowboy took his small Bible with one hand. He held reins and the Stetson he'd removed in the other. "I feel moved at this moment to read verse before we head out." It surprised him some when the Scriptures fell open at pages separated by some kind of dried leaf. Cowboy recognized it at last as Narrow Leaf Cottonwood. Brother Van had a stack of them piled on the cabin's side table. "I don't remember the preacher doing this," he told Dusty. "There must be a passage here in the Book of Luke he wanted me to read." Cowboy ran a long finger over the left page and halfway down the right.

The searching stopped when his eyes fell upon the words: "Return home and tell them how much God has done for you. So the man went away and told all over town how much Jesus had done for him."

Cowboy returned the hat to his head. He looked over a shoulder trying to spot the mountains they had descended from. At this distance, the peaks were barely a blur. The wrangler studied them anyway for a long moment. He could not imagine riding further north into the high snow country this late in the year. Certainly not doing so with such determined intention, but that was Brother Van's path, not his. He expected that his own would be the more difficult.

Cowboy heaved himself on Dusty's back. He used both hands on the saddle's horn and no stirrups, mounting up like some young buckaroo. "We don't need to ride the wagon tongue this time, *mi caballo*, to point rightly toward Atascosa County." He patted the buckskin's shoulder with a gentle touch. "Texas is that-a-way."

Cowboy nodded at the far horizon, turning the big horse until they headed south. Tapping a boot heel, he nudged Dusty to a canter.

They loped the trail at an easy pace.

Their journey home had begun.

Never Seen His Face
Study Questions

1. In this story, Cowboy encounters Jesus Christ in a dream. In the dream, Jesus knows Cowboy's given name, for he says that they are brothers, sons of God. Scripture says in 2 Timothy 2:19 that "the Lord knows those who are His." Can you say the same thing as Cowboy? Are you a brother of Christ? Do you know Him, and does He know you?

2. Cowboy's long and arduous quest to find Jesus is finally over, as he experiences Christ in a dream. God kept a promise to Cowboy that night, as found in Hebrews 11:6: "[God] is a rewarder of those who seek Him." If you haven't experienced God but are earnestly seeking the truth about Him, then God promises that He will reward your diligence. Are you seeking God in your own life? If you haven't come to that point in your path yet, what is keeping you from seeking to find God?

3. While not all spiritual experiences may be as dramatic as Cowboy's, any experience with Jesus Christ will impact one's life. For Cowboy, this meant that he would stop running from his past,

return to his family, and make amends. What is God asking you to do in your own life? Is there anything in your path that would hinder you from following God's call?

Call to Action

Dear Lord Jesus,

I know that I am a sinner,
and I ask for Your forgiveness.

I believe You died for my sins
and rose from the dead.

I turn from my sins and invite
You to come into my life.

I want to trust and follow
You as my Lord and Savior.

In Your Name.
Amen

Dusty's Song

I am an old range rider,
I follow the cattle trail—
Just me and my *caballo*,
Our journey's quite the tale.

I still rope and wrangle,
Can toss a steer with ease,
I spur my big horse Dusty—
To take me where I please.

About Cowboy Church

Cowboy churches are local Christian churches within the cowboy culture that are distinctively Western heritage in character. A typical cowboy church may meet in a rural setting in a barn, metal building, arena, sale barn, or old western building; have its own rodeo arena, and a country gospel band.

Baptisms are generally done in a stock tank. The sermons are usually short and simple, in order to better to be understood by the parishioners. Some cowboy churches have covered arenas where rodeo events such as bull riding, team roping, ranch sorting, team penning and equestrian events are held on weeknights.

Many cowboy churches have existed throughout the western states for the past forty or fifty years, however just in the past fifteen or so years has there been an explosion of growth within the "movement".

Prior to 1980 there were no less than 5 cowboy churches in Texas, now the number exceeds 200, and there are an estimated 750 nationwide. There has been no definitive group that established the movement; rather it seems to have had a spontaneous beginning in diverse areas of the country at nearly the same time.

Some of these cowboy churches are an outgrowth of ministries to professional rodeo or team roping events, while the roots of many can be traced back to ministry events associated with ranch rodeos, ranch horse competitions, chuck wagon cooking competitions, cowboy poetry gatherings and other "cowboy culture" events.

Excerpt from Book III

Dusty and the Cowboy:

Coming Home

All That Glitters

The newlyweds had no pigs when they came to this hilltop. It sat squatting at the edge of endless plains, spotted now with piles of winter drifts. The only thing the man's grandfather left him there was a low-slung badly weathered cabin. Chinking usually packed between solid logs had long since gone missing, as were doors, hinges, and some of the siding on the broken gable barn.

Starting late from the Maryland eastern shore, they had missed the summer with its opportunity to settle in without the overriding concern for the first snowfall or the sub-zero temperatures that always came with it. Arriving two days past the autumn equinox gave this couple precious little time to prepare the dilapidated abode for the cold or to lay in supplies enough to carry them to the spring. Quick arrangements had been bartered with a homesteader down the valley to provide them eight small pigs.

Now with the season's second snowfall just beginning, only four pigs still survived. On random evenings, panicked squeals in the darkness, drowned out by ferocious caterwauling, gave way to the next morning's discovered horror. Bloody, half-eaten, and grotesque to the point of night deliriums, the ravaged carcass indicated how easily the marauder had taken his prey. Tracks in the snow indicated a sizable mountain lion.

Not wanting their inexperience to cause their starvation before the snows could melt, Cowboy took it upon himself, unasked, to even out the odds.

                              * * *

The cougar stopped when he smelled the blood. In
another moment, he found the heap of rabbit guts
Cowboy had piled at the base of the tree. That the cat
gobbled down in big bites, as though famished. Light of
the full moon glistened off the snowy ground, and made
the feline's fur glow a tawny brown in the clear night.

For a long minute, a rough tongue licked its mouth
and chin to taste the last of this unexpected morsel. The
cat's nostrils continued to search for scent, and found
something of interest nearby; in the direction of the tree
top.

At a height of about eight feet Cowboy had nailed the
rabbit carcass into the tree's bark with a hand-forged
spike. Unsatisfied hunger, mixed with curiosity, made
the cougar raise up on hind legs to sniff at more easy
food just barely out of its paw's reach.

Next to the barn, Cowboy used the corral's top rail to
balance the Winchester. He steadied the sight at a spot at
the base of the skull, between and just below the cat's
cocked ears. The wrangler let his breath out slowly. He
could feel the curve of the trigger touching the tip of his
finger.

At this distance it would be hard to miss.

Introducing

Team Dusty

About the Author

T. W. Lawrence is a native Texan. Born at the edge of the Hill Country near San Antonio, his father was a successful veterinarian and his mother taught in the nearby junior high school.

Words — their meanings and origins — were always a topic of family conversation as T. W. grew up. Writing was a natural offshoot of his active imagination and capacity for poetic observations.

His long-time writing career has produced a portfolio that includes more than forty published articles, six professional course manuals, the short story anthology *Take Me To Texas*, and the novels, *Texas Cool Million* and *Tracks of the Sandman*.

He is a member of Christian Writers Guild, American Christian Fiction Writers, Western Writers of America, and Writers' League of Texas.

Jonathan Cooper
Master of Theological Studies

From an early age, Jonathan Cooper was an avid reader. His mother was a high school English teacher, and she instilled in him a deep-seated love and appreciation for the power of the written word. Jonathan enjoys writing and teaching, and he has a particular fondness for theological pursuits.

Jonathan received his formal theological training at Southwestern Baptist Theological Seminary in Fort Worth, Texas, and at Candler School of Theology, Emory University, in Decatur, Georgia. His graduate studies focused on biblical theology and the Hebrew Scriptures.

Jonathan currently serves at Johnson Ferry Baptist Church, in Marietta, GA, where he lives with his wife and three children. In his spare time, Jonathan is writing his first novel.

Moby
Moby in the Morning

Moby's alarm has been going off every weekday morning at 3:30 for the past 40 years and he loves it. It means he will soon be in front of the microphone doing what he does best - entertaining the thousands of members of his radio family across this great country.

Moby started his radio career at the age of 15 in Crossville, Tenn., his hometown and the place he got the nickname, Moby. Although he had other career plans, he was hooked. He enrolled in college with the idea of becoming a high school band director, but soon gave it up to pursue his dream of a radio career. From Nashville to Houston and Dallas to Atlanta, he's been an early-morning fixture for fans across the South.

For Moby, it's always been and will always be about the music, the listeners, and the country we ALL love.

It's that passion for what he does and the deep understanding of who his listeners are that have made him a proud member of the Country Radio Hall of Fame. He is also the five-time winner of Billboard's Major Market Country Morning Show of the Year and two-time nominee for the Major Market Morning Show of the Year by the CMA. He has also been honored as Academy of Country Music's Major Market DJ of the Year.

Moby shares his life with his third and favorite wife yet, Mary Beth, (she's told him that IF there's a fourth wife, it had better be a nurse with money) and his only female child, 10 year old daughter Grace, who can never date! They reside just outside of Atlanta, GA.

To connect with Moby, visit
www.mobyinthemorning.com

Sandy Weaver Carman
CEO, Voicework on Demand

Sandy Weaver Carman is the driving force behind Voicework on Demand, Inc., an audio production company specializing in audio book and audio learning production. Sandy spent her career on the radio, working in Atlanta, Washington DC, Boston and Columbus, GA. It was during her radio career that she fell in love with audio production, and in 2008, she decided to start a company. As a voice talent and audio editor, Sandy works with writers, coaches, trainers and speakers, helping them to create audio programs from their books, webinars and keynotes. Whether working with audio they provide or starting from scratch and talking their words, Sandy develops products for her clients that provide a revenue river – income from work they've already done.

As a writer, Sandy has article publishing credits going back to her teens, and she finally buckled down and wrote an entire book. "The Original MBA – Succeed in Business Using Mom's Best Advice" is a story-filled book of life lessons that help students, new hires and job-changers get a leg up in their careers. She's also written "Create a Revenue River," an e-book designed to help those who wish to create their own audio products. She's a sought-after speaker, wowing audiences with useable information packaged inside fun stories.

In her personal life, Sandy is married to Bob Carman, a long-time employee at IBM. He golfs, she tries, but her favorite sport is anything that can include their dogs. They have two Siberian Huskies, and Sandy is not just a competitor in conformation, obedience, agility and pack-hiking, she's a licensed AKC judge. Sandy is the Education Coordinator for the Siberian Husky Club of America and is a budding runner and tri-athlete. They live just outside of Atlanta, GA.

To connect with Sandy, visit
http://about.me/SandyWeaverCarman

Vanessa Lowry
Graphic Designer, Marketing Consultant, Radio Host

In addition to designing the covers for T.W. Lawrence's print and audio books, Vanessa creates marketing materials such as business cards, posters, and more.

Wearing her radio host hat, Vanessa interviewed T.W. on Write Here, Write Now and Art as Worship. Links to these show archives are available on www.Connect4Leverage.com.

T.W. talks about how Project Dusty evolved on Write Here,Write Now. After clicking on the page link for Write Here,Write Now Radio, scroll down to "Print and Audio…Leveraging Content."

On Art as Worship, T.W. discusses how creating the Dusty series transformed his own faith journey and continues to guide his spiritual path. Click the Art as Worship Radio link and find Walter (T.W.) Lawrence in the list of artists to access the 30-minute discussion.

Vanessa says, "I am grateful to be a member of Team Dusty and help T.W. bring his design and marketing ideas to life. I love the joy of collaborating with him."

Find out more about Vanessa and
the services she provides authors at
www.Connect4Leverage.com

Michael Belk
Journeys with the Messiah

Michael Belk's photography has appeared in Vogue, GQ and Vanity Fair for clients that include Nautica, J.Crew and others. A self-taught photographer, his career began in the fashion industry - first in retail, and then as a sales executive for a prestigious men's clothing line in the 60s and 70s. Then, photography snagged his soul.

Combining his gift for photography with a natural sense for sales and marketing, Michael began creating print collateral and, eventually, advertising campaigns throughout the clothing industry. With his unique style and quality of products, his business and his reputation grew. He has been the man behind the camera, the creative director and the account executive for his own boutique agency.

After 30 successful years, Michael sensed that God had even greater plans for him and he began to pursue an idea that he believes God put on his heart. In 2008, he put his career on hold to begin work on a collection of fine art photographs that would depict messages of Jesus - showing His relevance in our modern world. The project, Journeys with the Messiah, was first published in late 2009 and has since received accolades from around the world as God visually connect hearts to His Son.

The images have been produced as limited-edition fine art pieces, a coffee table book, behind the scenes DVD, posters and more. Michael travels to churches and other organizations to present the story of "his journey

with the Messiah" in an exciting audio/visual presentation.
An exhibit, film and more images are planned.

Explore the images at
www.JourneyswiththeMessiah.org

Coming Soon

From

T.W. Lawrence

Dusty and the Cowboy:
Coming Home

(2015)

Brewster and Bailey:
Teenage Buckaroos

(2016)

Dusty and the Cowboy

Audiobooks

Downloads:

Audible.com
iTunes

CDs:

Amazon

eBooks

Kindle
Nook
iTunes

Contact Information

www.facebook.com/DustyAndTheCowboy

DustyAndTheCowboy@gmail.com

www.DustyAndTheCowboy.com

www.ingramcontent.com/pod-product-compliance
Lightning Source LLC
Chambersburg PA
CBHW020619120726
47905CB00003B/862